*Pride Publishing books by Sarah Honey and L̶i̶s̶a̶ H̶*

**B**

G000080027

Hot Bite. Contractually Yours

# Hot Bite

# CONTRACTUALLY YOURS

## SARAH HONEY

Contractually Yours
ISBN # 978-1-80250-567-2
©Copyright Sarah Honey 2023
Cover Art by Kelly Martin ©Copyright July 2023
Interior text design by Claire Siemaszkiewicz
Pride Publishing

Published in 2023 by Pride Publishing, United Kingdom.

Pride Publishing is an imprint of Totally Entwined Group Limited.

# CONTRACTUALLY YOURS

# Dedication

For Steph and Nick, who only laughed at me a
little bit when I fell off my bike on Rottnest.

# Chapter One

*Submit Application*

The cursor sat unmoving over the box on his laptop screen as Nate bit his lip.

He could do this.

He *wanted* to do this. He'd done his research, and the Shiftercorp Companionship Programme, known as the SCP, was as squeaky clean as it could get without being suspiciously above board. It had been running for almost ten years, since a year after the global werewolf reveal, so it wasn't like he was worried for his safety.

The inevitable comparison to prostitution that the Programme drew wasn't what had him hesitating, either. Nate had never seen the Companionship Programme like that. As far as he was concerned, Shiftercorp was kind of like Grindr for shifters — both parties knew what to expect, and everyone walked away satisfied. It was big business, with a lot of shifters preferring a partner who'd consented to and was prepared for the rigours of shifter sex—which was, from all accounts, a wild ride, pun intended.

Nate *loved* sex, and he didn't believe there was anything wrong with monetising his talents in the bedroom. What was that saying about "find a job you love and never work a day in your life?" Sure, maybe whoever said it hadn't had being a shifter's paid fuck-buddy for the summer in mind, but that was beside the point.

And it wasn't the shifter factor—Nate had exactly zero objections to getting railed by a werewolf—or even, say, a bear.

Actually, he'd been railed by a bear more than once, but he suspected that it wasn't even close to the same thing.

Nate hadn't experienced shifter sex—yet—but he had friends who swore it was a whole other level of awesome, which made sense, given a shifter's increased speed, strength and stamina. The one thing stopping Nate had been lack of opportunity.

And on a more practical level, applying to the Companionship Programme meant that instead of working as a brickie's labourer and sweating his arse off mixing cement and building retaining walls in the heat of summer, he'd be getting paid for getting laid. It was a win-win situation.

So why couldn't he just...hit the button?

He ran a hand through his messy dark hair and spun in his office chair, catching sight of his reflection in the mirror as he did so. When he looked at the picture that he presented, he was able to admit to himself what the problem was.

He was scared he wouldn't make the cut.

The thing was, most of the applicants for the Companion Programme were eighteen-, nineteen- and twenty-year-olds — uni students looking to clear their HECS debts in one fell swoop. And there was a definite *type*. Instagram-pretty, with wide eyes, plump glossy lips, perky little tits on the girls and next to no body hair on the guys. Cute little werewolf snacks, every one of them, ready to be gobbled up by the big bad wolf.

Nate didn't fit that brief.

For starters, at twenty-four he was older than the norm, and he sported a decent amount of muscle, gained as a result of hauling bricks and sacks of mortar around for years. He was tan from working outdoors, with a light dusting of chest hair and a colourful half sleeve he'd gotten in Bali a few years back on his one overseas trip. His hair got a trim whenever he was near a barber and remembered, so it didn't exactly have a signature style. His skin-care products consisted of SPF 50+ sunscreen, and his beauty regimen was showering after work.

Instagram-pretty he was not.

He worried that even if he grew a pair and applied, they'd turn him down flat, and he wasn't sure his ego could take it. As long as the application sat on his laptop unsubmitted, he still had a chance. It was like not checking the lottery numbers — it meant he might still be a winner. Okay, fine. He'd admit that his logic was shaky on that one.

The point was, he wanted this — almost too much. *That* was why his application had been sitting completed on his laptop for the last three weeks, but he hadn't pushed the button yet.

Except he'd run out of time to dick about. The deadline to apply for this summer's intake was midnight tonight if he wanted to make the cut for the January round of selections. And while he made a decent enough wage, it would be nice not to have to worry about money, what with his old ute making weird noises every time he changed gear and his rent going up next month. Nate wanted to buy a place of his own, and this was the perfect opportunity to earn a deposit, because the SCP paid *big*.

He ran a hand through his hair again, regarded himself in the mirror and tried to think positive thoughts. Sure, maybe he didn't have delicate high cheekbones or obscenely long lashes and a pixie cut. Maybe he wasn't a dance student from the local Performing Arts Academy who could bend in half and lick his own arsehole, but there must be werewolves who weren't into that whole delicate, waify thing?

Objectively, Nate knew he was decent looking, with deep brown eyes and dark hair that had a hint of a curl when left to its own devices. He'd been told he was hot more than once, and he never seemed to have any trouble finding someone to bring home for the night. Plus, he had a decent-sized dick, and he knew how to use it. That had to count for something, right?

He put on his best smile. "You're not just a werewolf snack," he told himself, "you're the entire fucking buffet."

And yeah, when he looked at the face in the mirror, he had to agree that he was.

Before he could change his mind, he spun in his chair and hit the enter key. The screen blinked, and a message appeared.

*Thank you for your application. We will be in contact in the next seven to ten working days.*

Nate let out a loud breath, and the tension he hadn't known he was carrying left him in a rush. For better or for worse, he was doing this.

\* \* \* \*

Nate got a reply the next afternoon. He was checking his emails on his phone during smoko while he looked across the highway at the Indian Ocean. Working on site across from Hilary's Beach Harbour wasn't the bonus most people assumed it was. Sure, the view was nice, but unless the sea breeze was in, it was just a tease, a reminder that other people were spending their days surfing and swimming and walking their dogs instead of working.

That was another reason he'd applied as a Companion—even if he spent the entire month of January as a companion having super-athletic sex with a werewolf, it would *still* be easier on his body than being a brickie's labourer during an Australian summer.

It *would* most likely be a werewolf partner—they made up the majority of the shifter population, followed by felines, and after careful consideration, he'd omitted cat shifters from his selection criteria. Just *thinking* about barbed penises had him squirming.

He opened the email, assuming it was just an acknowledgement of his application, but then he read the words, *"We are pleased to welcome you to the Shiftercorp Companionship Programme. Please find attached..."*

His breath caught. It looked like a Perth tradie who wasn't Instagram-pretty but who had muscles and ink and a tan gained from working outdoors might have what it took, after all.

"You right, Nate?" his boss, Sully, asked. "You look like you've seen a ghost."

Nate remembered how to breathe. "Yeah. Just..." He debated if it was too soon to say anything or if he should wait until he had more details, but Sully had given him a job right out of school, and he'd always been a decent bloke. He hadn't so much as blinked when he found out Nate was gay, and he'd never once laid him off, even when work had been tight. The least Nate could do was give him a heads up that he might need a new offsider. "I might need time off, over the next month."

Sully creased his brow. "Everything okay?"

"I applied to the SCP and I got in," Nate blurted.

Sully raised his eyebrows. "Really? You never said you were applying."

"Yeah. I didn't think I had a chance, so I didn't mention it, but it looks like I'm in."

He hoped Sully wouldn't try to talk him out of it, but the man just pulled off his hard hat and swiped his brow with a forearm, spreading cement dust across his skin, and said, "Good for you. When do you start? My nephew's been after me for some hours over his uni break, so the timing might work."

Nate cleared his throat. "I dunno. I've just been accepted." He read the email again, paying more attention to the details this time. "I have to screen the candidates and see who I like, and then they, um. Bid on me." His face heated at the thought of it.

Sully broke into a grin. "You're hot property, huh?" He extended his arms and clasped his hands in front of himself, planted his feet and started doing a weird sort of hip gyration that was no doubt meant to be sexy, all while chanting, "Bow chicka bow-wow." It was hilarious and disturbing all at once. Nate snorted with laughter. "Stop it. You're scaring the seagulls." He'd expected some ribbing, because it did sound ridiculous, being bid on as 'entertainment' for single, wealthy werewolves—but in fact it was big business. Nate knew that he could expect to make thousands of dollars, for just a few weeks' work. For that, he could put up with Sully taking the piss.

\* \* \* \*

There was a certain set of pearl-clutchers who liked to compare the SCP recruitment process to human trafficking, and they were painfully vocal about it. But a happy side effect of the Puritans and their protests was that the Shifter community was almost fanatical about there being not so much of a hint of coercion regarding partnerships through the SCP—which meant that when it came to deciding who he was willing to sleep with, Nate was the one calling the shots.

The initial match-ups were all done via an online profile, but when he met his selection in person, if they weren't a good fit, he could change his mind and choose someone else, no harm, no foul. And if at any time during his contract he wanted to walk away from the whole thing he could, and he'd still be paid a pro-rata amount for the time he'd worked.

He got to choose who he'd accept as a partner, how long the contract ran for, and what he would and wouldn't be willing to do. He'd rejected fisting, figging and watersports right off the bat, as well as a heap of other stuff—some of which he'd googled to find out what it was and immediately wished he hadn't.

It was a pretty sweet deal that was geared towards enthusiastic participation. Nate could see why people were willing to jump through all the hoops that were needed just to apply. Hell, he'd jumped through them himself, hadn't he? His least favourite bit had been the mandatory pre-application medical—that shit had been more intimate than some dates he'd been on.

Still, it had been worth it.

Now that he'd been accepted, things moved fast—faster than he'd expected. Nate was sent the profiles of shifters who had expressed an interest in him, and they were all werewolves. He received links to dozens of files so he could give a tick of approval to the ones he liked, and he had to admit, the amount of interest was flattering. It took half a day of going over the profiles while he sat on his bed, laptop balanced on his knees and his ceiling fan going full tilt in an effort to combat the heat, before he managed to narrow it down to just five.

Some people were of the opinion that approving more bidders was better because it encouraged a higher final pay-out, but Nate was more cautious in his choices. He wanted whoever won his services to be someone he could spend the entire summer with, which meant that for him, they needed to tick his boxes when it came to physical attraction. Just because he was getting paid for it didn't mean he didn't want to enjoy the sex as well.

Still, Nate couldn't help laughing at himself. He'd always claimed he didn't have a type, yet when the five bidder profiles were lined up across the screen, every single one of them was, for want of a better term, a silver fox. Or silver wolf, maybe? Regardless, his preferences were showing. Older, taller, stubbled and with a rugged vibe. And every last one of them had a steely glint in their eyes that said they knew what they liked and weren't afraid to ask for it.

He wondered if he shouldn't check the profiles again in case there was someone who *wasn't* older than him, but in the end, he decided *fuck it*.

These were the men whose photos made his dick throb. He couldn't wait to see if they'd do the same when he met them in the flesh.

\* \* \* \*

Nate checked the zip on his bag one last time, scanned his bedroom for anything he might need in the next week, and, with a final look around, pulled the door shut behind him and made his way to the limousine parked at the kerb.

It was starkly out of place in Balga, the gleam of the sun off the polished paintwork a stark contrast to the peeling paint of Nate's front door. He fought the urge to apologise to the driver when he ducked into the back seat. But Liz, the werewolf liaison officer he'd been dealing with so far, didn't comment on the neighbourhood, just gave Nate a small smile and handed him a cold bottle of water from the mini bar. He took it with a grateful nod, pressing it against his forehead for a second before draining it in one go.

He was sweating his balls off in this suit, but the instructions from his winning bidder had been clear. Formal dress for their first meeting. And for the amount that Nate was being offered for his companionship, he figured he could cope with a day's discomfort.

Nate had found it unreal, the concept of werewolves bidding against each other for *him*, but after submitting his acceptable candidates, he'd received an email informing him that after something of a bidding war, someone had paid for the opportunity to spend a week with him — the 'and fuck him stupid' was implied. The bidder had also asked for the option to extend the contract for up to a month. If that option was passed on, Nate still got a bonus for making himself available.

Bidder D973 — Nate wouldn't learn his potential partner's identity until they met — was willing to pay an obscene amount for the week and the renewal option, which was pretty bloody flattering — but also, it was enough for Nate to replace his dying ute and still have a decent chunk left put a deposit on a place of his own in one of the nicer areas. It was unreal, looking at properties in Floreat, knowing that now they weren't forever out of reach.

As long as he and D973 hit it off at today's meeting and got the paperwork squared away, Nate could be leaving with his werewolf by the end of the day — and given what he'd seen on the guy's profile, Nate was certain they *would* hit it off, because his bidder was the stuff of wet dreams.

Thus, the luggage.

He tapped a nervous staccato with his shoe against the floor of the limo before catching himself and stopping. Werewolves had sensitive hearing, and he didn't think Liz would appreciate his tap-tap-tapping. He managed to keep himself in check for the rest of the ride, and it wasn't long before they pulled up in front of the Ritz-Carlton. He huffed out a breath and Liz leaned across and put a hand on his knee. "If you're having second thoughts, now's the time to say so."

"No second thoughts. Just nerves."

She raised a disbelieving eyebrow. "Your heartbeat says otherwise." Right. Nate had forgotten that to a werewolf, he was an open book. "Will it help if I tell you that most companions regard this as a positive experience? In fact, plenty of them sign up more than once. I had one client who worked five summers and then retired to Bali."

Nate nodded, grateful for the reassurance. His racing heart slowed down a bit. He was going to do this. He was going to have the time of his life riding werewolf dick, and he was going to get *paid* for it. There was no downside to this arrangement. He took a deep breath and stepped out of the car. Time to meet the guy who would own his arse — literally — for the next week.

He followed Liz inside, his duffle bag slung over one shoulder, out of place in the luxurious surroundings that were all floor-to-ceiling timber and marble and gilt. He craned his neck, taking in what looked like giant glass test tubes suspended from the ceiling as Liz steered them through reception. He guessed it was someone's idea of art.

They left the enormous foyer behind and came to a meeting room, where Liz deposited Nate at the conference table. Her phone rang and she looked at the screen, her brow creasing. "I have to take this. Please wait here and I'll be right back." As she stepped outside, Nate heard her say, "Yes, sir. We've just arrived. No, not yet."

Nate looked around. The room was a cookie-cutter hotel meeting space, albeit a *swanky* cookie-cutter hotel space. There was the expected long timber table and chairs surrounding it, and carpeting with a blue and white pattern. There was a pitcher of iced water, a fancy table runner and an abstract print of what might have been the ocean on the wall.

He poured himself a glass of water and when five minutes became ten, he gave in and checked his phone, just so he wouldn't freak out. He was busy scrolling when the door opened and Liz came back in. She cleared her throat and looked everywhere except at him. "Nathan...there's been a slight change of plans."

He pocketed his phone and sat up straight. "They haven't bailed, have they?" Despite his earlier nerves, he found he was more disappointed by the thought that he might not get his week as a werewolf fuckbuddy than he'd expected.

Liz swallowed. "The thing is" — she twisted her hands together — "there was a glitch with the original winning bid. The contract will still go ahead as agreed," she hastened to add. "You'll just have a...different partner."

Her body was a line of tension, and Nate felt a stab of pity for her at having to be the bearer of bad news. He decided that he wasn't going to be the one to make her day worse. "So, I'm just hooking up with a different bidder? No big deal. Shit happens, right?"

Besides, it *wasn't* a big deal. D973 had been the favourite of his selections, true, and Nate had been looking forward to spending a week with him, but it wasn't the end of the world. "Which one of my selections is the lucky guy now?"

Liz took a deep breath. "That's the thing. The winner isn't *technically* on your list of approved bidders. But his bid is still valid."

Nate took a second to consider that, and stood and turned so he was facing her. "What do you mean, he's not technically on my list? I thought your system was meant to be fool-proof?"

"And up until now it has been. And the winner *is* ID number D973. It's just...the profile that was listed doesn't belong to him. Somehow, D973 was assigned to two bidders."

The way Liz was fidgeting gave Nate the impression this was all kinds of bullshit. He caught her gaze and held it. "Liz? What aren't you telling me? Is this guy some sort of psycho who's hacked the system? Am I going to end up at the bottom of a well, rubbing the lotion on its skin?"

That startled a laugh out of her, which was somewhat reassuring. "No, it's nothing like that."

"Is he ninety-five, bald and smells like Dencorub? Are there dentures? Because that might be a hard limit."

Liz shook her head, and Nate was glad to see that her shoulders were no longer pulled up quite so high around her ears. "It's none of those things, I promise. And this applicant *does* match your preferred type, based on who you selected."

"Oh?" That caught Nate's interest.

"Oh, yes. In fact, if it hadn't been for the system hiding his profile, I'm confident you would have selected him." She bit her lip. "Perhaps you could talk with him, and see what you think? He's very eager to meet you."

Nate considered saying no for a split second, but what did he have to lose? "Fine. I'll meet him."

Liz gave a relieved smile. "Excellent. Follow me."

Nate paused where he stood. "Wait, where are we going?"

"Mr Hudson has asked that we meet him in his suite."

Nate baulked, folding his arms over his chest. "Nope. That's not how it's done. First meetings are always public meeting spaces. No hotel rooms. Those are the rules."

"It's fine, I promise," Liz said, with something like desperation in her voice. "Please?"

Nate almost said no. *Almost.* But he'd always trusted his gut, and he wasn't getting any kind of serial killer or kidney-stealing accomplice vibe from Liz. It was more like she was trying to keep somebody very, very important happy. "This guy, is he...special? Like, the big werewolf cheese or something?" He couldn't think of any other reason for her to suggest the break in protocol.

"Or something," Liz said, biting her lip. "The normal rules tend not to apply where Mr Hudson is concerned. But I promise you, Nathan, it's all above board. And you're still free to say no."

A sensible person might have turned and walked away, but Nate's curiosity was piqued now. And Liz's reminder that he *could* say no meant he didn't feel like he needed to. Besides, it wasn't like he was going in alone. He squared his shoulders. "Fine. Let's go meet your werewolf Howard Hughes. But I'm expecting you to make sure everything's above board, and also to leap in and use your claws to defend me if he *is* a serial killer."

"I will," Liz said, "but he's not." Still, her eyes flashed gold, and Nate found it more reassuring than he wanted to admit.

Liz wasted no time leading the way to the elevators, and shepherded Nate inside like she was afraid he might change his mind, and before long they were standing in front of a door on the top floor. Liz knocked, and a deep, velvety voice called, "Enter."

*Fuck.* If this guy looked anything like he sounded, Nate was one hundred percent going to sleep with him—even if he *did* end up at the bottom of a well.

Liz swiped a key card and opened the door. Nate followed her inside. He was greeted by the sight of a tall, broad figure with his back to them, looking out through the floor-to-ceiling windows at the Perth cityscape. Threads of afternoon sunlight glinted off dark blond hair that brushed the collar of the man's shirt in a way that suggested the length was a deliberate choice. He had wide shoulders that tapered down to a trim waist and long, long legs. One hand was in his pocket, which pulled the fabric of his suit pants in a way that highlighted thick thighs and a stunning arse.

Nate barely had a moment to wonder if the mysterious Mr Hudson was this attractive from every angle before the man himself turned, and Nate almost forgot how to breathe.

*Seriously, who gave this guy permission to be that good looking?*

Mr Hudson looked to be somewhere in his thirties—although with werewolves, it was almost impossible to guess—and he was younger than Nate's other selections, but he exuded an air of authority. The way he looked Nate up and down, like he was starving and Nate was the main course, almost had Nate's knees buckling under him with a sudden urge to submit, to bare his throat to this stranger.

The man's blond hair was threaded with the slightest hints of silver, which for Nate, added a whole other layer of *hnnngh* to his appeal. Hazel eyes sparkled with mischief and — *Lord have mercy* — when he smiled, his pleasure at Nate's appearance obvious, the corners of them crinkled in a way that should be illegal for reasons of excessive hotness.

His smile made the werewolf look almost rakish, revealing perfect teeth and a dimple in one cheek, just above his carefully sculpted stubble. He had a killer jawline, and Nate lost focus for a second there as he envisioned kissing all along it and nibbling at the pretty ears peeking out from under that glorious hair.

He snapped back to attention when the man stepped forward, his smile sharpening into something well, wolfish, that promised one hell of a good time. He extended a broad palm. "Nathan, I take it?" he asked, his voice a sultry burr.

"That's, yeah. I am. Me." Nate took his hand, and even the strength and heat of the man's grip was enough to have his heart beating faster and his dick perking up. "And you're…D973?"

The man let out a low chuckle, and Nate held back a groan. That voice was going to be the death of him.

"Call me Cooper. If we're going to do this, I think we should be on a first name basis." He raised one eyebrow and leaned in close, placing one hand on Nate's shoulder. It was the most erotic innocent touch Nate had ever experienced. "That is, if you haven't been put off by the unconventional circumstances?"

*This man. Fuck.*

He was everything Nate had ever wanted in a man — suave, gorgeous and charming — and from the way he kept looking Nate up and down, his tongue tracing his bottom lip, the attraction was mutual.

Nate wanted nothing more than to kiss him and see if that stubble felt as good as he suspected it would brushing against his skin, but Liz was still hovering, hands fluttering as she cleared her throat. Nate knew she was going to interject with rules and provisos and reminders—just like he'd asked her to. And while under normal circumstances Nate would be all about that, right now he was desperate to see what was hiding under Cooper Hudson's suit, run his hands all over him, and maybe lick him from head to foot.

He shot Liz a look that he hoped said *do not ruin this for me,* and before he could overthink it, said, "Yeah, we're doing this. You can call me Nate."

# Chapter Two

Cooper Hudson knew he should feel bad for playing
the system, but looking at the young man in front of
him with his messy dark hair, wide eyes and kissable
mouth, he couldn't bring himself to regret what he was
about to do.

Never once in the past five years had he used his
position to step outside the parameters, bend the rules
or mess with the bidding process. But then, nobody had
caught his eye in quite the way that Nathan Watson
had.

Somewhere along the line after the launch of
Shiftercorp Companions, it seemed that potential
applicants had discovered that there was a tendency
amongst werewolves to choose partners who had a
smaller build than them. That had somehow morphed
into a universally accepted truth that *all* werewolves
wanted their companions to be slender, delicate
creatures. The result had been a wave of applicants
who fit that sylph-like, dainty stereotype perfectly —

which was fine. A lot of the werewolves who signed up for a companion *did* love that.

But Cooper found that the parade of pretty little things just didn't do it for him. The applicants all had a terrible sort of sameness to them, like the contestants in toddler beauty pageants. There was no way to know what they were like underneath the layers of Photoshop, filtering and spray tan. In fact, although he didn't advertise it, Cooper had never bothered with a companion. It wasn't that he was uninterested, so much as he hadn't been tempted to indulge.

His job kept him busy enough that it wasn't practical to take weeks at a time off just to scratch an itch, but another part of it, as outdated as it seemed, was that Cooper wasn't comfortable taking just anyone to bed — or rather, his *wolf* wasn't.

Cooper's shifter side had definite preferences.

So when Nathan Watson's profile picture had popped up on Cooper's screen with a query about the credit rating of bidder D973 and it had made Cooper's wolf sit up and take notice, that in itself was rare enough that he'd decided to investigate further.

He'd clicked on Nathan's complete profile to see what was sparking such interest. When he'd opened the full gallery of photos, he'd found himself unable to look away, intrigued. There had been something about Nathan, with his imperfectly styled hair and hint of stubble. Maybe it was the tan, muscled forearms, or the hint of ink peeking out of Nathan's cuffed shirtsleeves or perhaps it was the wide, open smile that lit up his face. Whatever it was, Nathan had struck Cooper as someone *real*.

Cooper — and his wolf — had wanted him, plain and simple.

So, ignoring his own rules, he'd made some calls. In a stroke of luck, it turned out that D973 was, in fact, ineligible to bid, due to an unfortunate bitcoin encounter that had left them insolvent, and for the first time ever, Cooper had taken advantage of his position within Shiftercorp. Instead of allowing the option for Nathan's company to pass on to the next-highest bidder as per the usual operational protocols, strings had been pulled, a computer glitch manufactured, a profile and bid uploaded, and just like that, Cooper had *become* D973 — the director's cut, so to speak.

After that, it had just been a matter of flying from Sydney to Perth and hoping that Nathan Watson could be convinced to take a chance on a complete stranger.

Given the way Nathan was looking at him right now, it seemed Cooper's gamble had paid off.

Liz cleared her throat and squared her shoulders. "The guidelines state that the first meeting is chaperoned."

"Yeah, nah. We're past that, Liz," Nathan said, his gaze fixed on Cooper in a way that made Cooper's wolf perk up. "First meeting's done."

"Agreed," Cooper said, the hint of a growl in his voice. "We don't need an audience for whatever happens next."

"But what about the contract? It has to be signed," Liz said. Cooper could sense the determination radiating from her — she was the head of West Coast Operations for a reason — and she was right, of course. The formalities had to be completed. After all, the cornerstones of the success of the SCP were visible, *enthusiastic* consent from the human employees, and impeccable paperwork.

So instead of backing Nathan up against a wall and nuzzling his throat like he wanted to, Cooper dropped his hand from Nathan's shoulder and stepped back with a sigh. "Of course. Nathan—I mean, Nate—are you happy with the standard contract?"

"Where do I sign?" Nate said, his gaze roving over Cooper's body. Cooper could feel the chemistry crackling between them. He hadn't *ever* been this drawn to someone, and he was thrilled that the attraction was mutual.

Liz led them over to the small desk in the corner of the suite and Nate almost snatched the pen from her in his eagerness. Once he'd signed, Nate turned and handed Cooper the pen, eyes wide and lips parted. Cooper wanted nothing more than to lick into that mouth and taste his new partner.

But first things first.

He signed his name with a flourish and Liz looked between them with a knowing smile. "If you don't need me for anything else, I'll go and file this." She wasted no time scooping up her copies of the paperwork and heading out of the door, then Cooper was left alone with his new boy.

He took a half-step forward so he was almost toe to toe with Nate, so close that he could see a smattering of freckles across the bridge of his nose and smell the fresh mint of his toothpaste. He leaned in and, like he'd wanted to since Nate had walked in the door, buried his face in the crook of his throat, inhaling deeply. Nate's breathing was fast, and Cooper could hear his heart racing, but his sensitive werewolf nose didn't pick up any traces of fear in his scent. No, Nate smelled of nothing except anticipation and pure, unbridled *lust*.

Cooper could relate.

Nate let out a shaky breath. "That...should not be as hot as it is." He half-moaned, tilting his head to one side.

"Uh-huh." Cooper licked a stripe up Nate's throat, lifted his head, and grinned. "Want me to stop, baby?"

"I didn't say that." Nate reached up and fumbled with the knot of his tie, and Cooper congratulated himself on giving instructions for Nate to wear a suit. Well-dressed young men were a personal weakness. While he'd suspected that Nate would scrub up well if given the chance, just *how* nicely he filled out his suit was an unexpected bonus. Of course, the downside was that now he was wearing far too many clothes for Cooper's liking.

He placed a hand over Nate's and helped tug the knot of his tie loose, slipping it over his head and flicking the top two buttons of his shirt open. The action released a wave of salt, sweat and heat from Nate's body into the air. It was intoxicating. Cooper dropped the tie, then slid his hands inside Nate's jacket and onto his hips, holding him in place as he leaned in and, reining in the wolf part of him that wanted to *claim, devour, consume,* placed a gentle kiss on that plush, soft mouth.

Nate froze at the first touch of Cooper's lips, but then he wrapped his arms around Cooper and kissed him back, fierce and passionate. Nate probed at the seam of Cooper's mouth, seeking entrance with his tongue, and rocked his hips forward, his erection obvious. He slid one hand around and clutched Cooper's arse, sending sparks up his spine.

*Huh. So much for taking it slow.*

Cooper smiled at the small triumph then opened his mouth to let Nate in, their tongues sliding against each other. Nate was right—this was far hotter than it should have been. They hadn't even made it to the bedroom, and already Cooper's cock was throbbing and his wolf was clamouring for *more, mine, now*. It took every scrap of his self-control to pull back, but Cooper hadn't made it to where he was today by being rash.

He ended the kiss and took a step backward, running a hand through his hair. He let out a long breath. "So, how far are you willing to take this today?" He hoped he didn't sound as desperate as he was, but he suspected the rasp in his voice gave him away.

Nate's eyes were bright, and his lips were kiss-plump and swollen. He stepped back into Cooper's space, one hand trailing down Cooper's chest and coming to rest on his abs. "I want... God, I want anything you'll give me."

Relief and anticipation coursed through Cooper at the same time. "Anything?"

Nate nodded, and his throat bobbed as he swallowed. "Yeah." He leaned in, and Cooper took the hint and kissed him again, nipping at Nate's bottom lip and savouring the moan it earned him. He slid one hand into Nate's hair to hold him in place, and he didn't miss the way Nate's arousal spiked when he gave a gentle tug to his curls.

Nate's mouth was all plush heat, and his scent was a heady mix of sweat and arousal. It wasn't long before Cooper's wolf was whining, insisting that kissing wasn't enough. Cooper broke the kiss. "Ready for more, baby?"

"Uh-huh." Nate nodded, and Cooper smirked at his glazed expression—although in truth, he was sure that if he checked the mirror, he'd see the same look reflected back. Everything about Nate was addictive, and Cooper wanted more of him.

He slipped his hands under the shoulders of Nate's jacket and guided him out of it, dropping it over the arm of a chair and running his hands up and down over Nate's chest. The muscles jumped under his touch.

He'd wanted to take it slow, peel Nate out of his suit like a sort of sexy unboxing, but he found he didn't possess that kind of patience. "Need you naked," he said, his voice hoarse with want.

Nate's breathing sped up and he reached out and tugged at Cooper's suit jacket. "Same. I can't wait to see what you're hiding under here."

There was a moment where they stood frozen, then there was a flurry of motion as Nate yanked Cooper's jacket off and flung it across the room before unbuttoning his own shirt and shucking out of it.

"Oh, baby. You're all kinds of perfect, aren't you?" Cooper breathed, awestruck.

Nate was *gorgeous*. He had well-muscled pecs, and the barbell through one nipple had Cooper's mouth watering with the need to latch onto it and tug until Nate begged — whether for more or for mercy, Cooper didn't care.

Nate's cheeks flushed pink. "I'm not perfect."

"Oh, I beg to differ, gorgeous boy." Cooper reached out and grazed a thumb over the piercing. "Got any more surprises like this for me?"

Nate shivered at his touch. "Just that one. I was going to get both done but it stung like a bitch."

"Worth it, from where I'm standing." Cooper gave in to the urge to give the metal bar an experimental tug.

Nate groaned. "Fuck, do that again."

"Oh, I will. I plan to touch you all over, baby." He could see it now—Nate naked and begging, and Cooper touching and tasting every inch of that tan skin, kissing along the ink of his tattoo. His cock hardened further at the thought.

Nate had kicked off his shoes and was fumbling with his belt, and Cooper wasted no time following his example in a race to feel Nate's bare skin against his own. He paused, though, when Nate pushed his suit pants and underwear down and stepped out of them. His cock, long and thick, sprang up and slapped against his belly. Nate was uncut, and the sight of the tip of his cock peeking out of his foreskin, rosy and inviting, had Cooper's breath catching.

He'd planned to spend some time getting to know Nate before coaxing him into bed in a slow, smooth seduction—but as soon as Nate had stepped into his presence, that idea had gone out of the window. There had been an immediate, tangible attraction between them, a pull that was nothing short of hypnotic.

It was almost impossible to resist, and Cooper wasn't even going to try. He didn't quite know *what* had come over him, but he did know *who* he wanted to come over him—namely, Nate. He dropped his shirt on the floor, then dropped to his knees right next to it. He needed that cock in his mouth, *right now*. "Fuck, baby. Can I taste you?"

Nate went wide-eyed, his cheeks staining pink, and his cock bobbed against his stomach. A drop of pre-cum welled up and dripped from the head, and Cooper didn't bother waiting for a reply, instead leaning in and giving a long, slow lick. Nate tasted of clean skin, musk and salt, and Cooper gave another lick, hungry for more, before taking the head in his mouth.

Nate whimpered, his hips rocking forward, and Cooper wrapped his hands around the back of his thighs and held him in place. The coarseness of leg hair against his palms and the soft velvet of dick skin against his tongue was a heady contrast, one that had his own cock straining in his suit pants.

He fucking *loved* giving head.

He swallowed Nate's cock down farther, savouring the fresh bursts of pre-cum on his tongue as he sucked and bobbed and licked. Nate let out a series of desperate noises that only spurred him on. Cooper didn't hesitate to use every trick he knew to bring Nate closer to the edge, and it wasn't long before Nate tangled one hand in his hair and gave a sharp tug. "Oh, fuck, I'm gonna —"

Cooper grinned around a mouthful of cock. He pulled off with a wet pop, wrapping a hand around Nate's shaft and working it, mesmerised by the slide of soft skin over hard flesh and the scent of desperation and pre-cum. "Gonna come on my face, baby?" he rasped out. "Paint me pretty, Nate?"

"Oh, fuck," Nate gasped, his hips stuttering and the hand in Cooper's hair tightening. *"Fuck."* He let out a low grunt as his cock throbbed against Cooper's palm, and Cooper closed his eyes just in time for the first streaks of cum to land on his face and across his lips, wet and warm and the best kind of filthy.

He swiped his tongue across his bottom lip to catch the flavour of his lover, and *oh*, he wanted more. He leaned forward, guiding Nate's still pulsing cock into his mouth, and eased him through the last of his orgasm, groaning at the delicious richness of Nate's release.

He could have stayed there all day, rolling in the scent and taste of his boy, but Nate let out a broken whine and tugged at his hair again, trembling.

He pulled off and pressed a soft kiss to the crease of Nate's thigh. Nate stumbled backward and collapsed into one of the armchairs in the suite.

Cooper couldn't suppress the curl of satisfaction in his gut when he took in Nate's dazed, fucked-out expression. "You like that, baby?"

Nate let out a shaky laugh. "I mean, obviously. Wow." He blinked, his gaze locking on the obvious bulge in Cooper's trousers. He licked his lips. "Please tell me I can return the favour?"

Like Cooper was going to refuse an invitation like that.

He rose to his feet with a sinuous grace, coming to stand in the vee of Nate's sprawled-out legs and reaching down to rub a thumb over his bottom lip. Nate gave a shy grin before he sucked Cooper's thumb into his mouth, looking up at him through thick dark lashes. Cooper's balls tightened just at the prospect of seeing those plump lips stretched around his dick.

"Fuck, Nate." He pulled his hand back and unzipped his pants, shoving them halfway down his thighs, underwear and all, exposing his erection. He was so hard he ached. When Nate opened his mouth and leaned forward, his breath hot against Cooper's skin, he had to grip the base of his cock and take a couple of deep breaths just to stop himself blowing his load there and then. When he felt like he wasn't going to embarrass himself, he guided the tip towards Nate's parted lips, his blood thrumming in anticipation.

He pushed into the hot, wet cavern of Nate's mouth, and *fuck*, whatever Cooper had agreed to pay Nate, he was going to double it because he'd never felt anything like this. Heat raced up his spine as Nate mouthed at his length, flicking his tongue over the head and working one hand into the space between Cooper's thighs and playing with his balls, fingertips teasing at the sensitive skin in a way that had Cooper throwing his head back and fighting the urge to drop his fangs and *howl*.

Instead he gripped at Nate's bare shoulders and held on, rocking forward and fucking into his mouth in short, urgent strokes. Nate, for his part, tipped his head back just enough that Cooper could slide further down his throat. The tiny, gasping noises he made were music to Cooper's ears.

Cooper knew it wasn't going to take much — his nerves tingled and his balls were heavy with the need for release. He moved one hand to the back of Nate's head, holding him in place, letting out a series of grunts in time with his thrusts, until he had to force himself to still his hips so he could pant out, "You gonna swallow for me, baby?"

Nate's response was to take him down to the root, gazing up at him through damp eyelashes as he sucked harder, cheeks hollowing. He tugged at Cooper's balls just right — and fuck, that was it, Cooper was *done*.

His spine arched and he gripped the back of Nate's head as he shot his load, white noise filling his brain and colours bursting behind his eyelids. His cock swelled in response to the way Nate's throat muscles convulsed around him when he swallowed. Cooper couldn't help thrusting forward, forcing himself deeper as he pumped another burst of cum down Nate's willing throat.

His fangs itched with the need to drop—and he *let* them, feeling his transformation roll over him, unwilling to hold it back. *Christ.* It must have been twenty years since he'd had sex so good it had made the wolf come out.

He slumped forward, relaxing his grip on Nate when his cock had spilled the last of his release. A low growl made its way out of his throat, echoing loud in the room, and Nate's breathing hitched as he pulled off Cooper's softening cock. He looked up at Cooper, eyes wide, and whispered, "Oh, wow. You shifted."

*Shit.*

The wolf was a lot to handle, and Cooper tilted his head back and closed his eyes, inwardly cursing. *Fuck.* He'd shown too much of himself, too soon.

Except when he glanced down again, Nate didn't look afraid or overwhelmed. He was grinning, more awestruck than anything. He licked his lips, catching the traces of Cooper's cum there, and said, "Fuck, that's hot."

# Chapter Three

Nate stared at the man—wolf?—at *Cooper*, and wondered if it was weird that instead of freaking out at Cooper's appearance, he was even more turned on by it.

Because Cooper the businessman, with his suit and his swagger and his voice like velvet and gravel? Abso-bloody-lutely magnificent. But Cooper the *wolf*, with glowing eyes, sharp fangs, pointed ears and a growl that could shake the earth?

He was perfection, and everything Nate had never known he'd wanted.

Of course, that could just have been his post-orgasm brain talking—which was also the reason he'd blurted out what he had.

Fuck, he hoped it wasn't offensive to find someone's werewolf form hot. He wasn't fetishising Cooper, was he? But if that was the case, was Cooper fetishising *Nate* and his humanity?

Was it fetishising someone to find both the human *and* the shifter aspect of them attractive?

And why was *fetishising* such a weird fucking word? Cooper was looking down at Nate and there was a glint of amusement in his eye, so Nate guessed he hadn't crossed any lines. "So, you think my wolf is hot?" Cooper sounded more curious than anything. He extended a hand—and yes, there were claws there, dark-tipped, razor-sharp and dangerous. Nate wondered what it said about him that his heart tripped in his chest and his pulse raced at the sight.

Nate took the hand between his own, drawing a fingertip down the back of Cooper's fingers one by one, tracing the tips of those wickedly sharp claws. "Yeah, I like the wolf. Is that a problem?"

Cooper laughed, low and deep with a hint of a growl underneath. "Trust me, it's the opposite of a problem." Cooper closed his eyes, and when he opened them, they were back to their regular colour. His extra teeth and pointed ears disappeared, vanishing back to wherever they went when they weren't needed. Nate was almost sad to see them go, but then Cooper smiled, his eyes lighting up and those adorable crinkles appearing at their edges, and Nate was reminded that *both* versions of Cooper were smoking hot.

Cooper bent and scooped up his shirt from the floor then wiped the worst of the cum off his face. He gripped Nate's hand and helped him to his feet. "Some things are better without fangs," he murmured, before tugging Nate in close and kissing him. It was the opposite of the needy, urgent kisses from earlier, soft and sweet, but it was still enough to take Nate's breath away.

When he pulled back, Cooper gave a lazy smile. "That was amazing, baby." He raised an eyebrow. "Did you enjoy it?"

"Saying I enjoyed it is an understatement," Nate said with a grin. "Except, it seems kind of unfair that you're still dressed. I'd like to see the whole package, not just your, well, package."

Cooper gave another one of his sultry smiles, one that made Nate want to swoon. "Well, you only had to ask." He shimmied out of his suit pants and underwear before kicking them off, and Nate got to see him naked.

And wow, it was a hell of a sight.

Cooper was all compact muscle and tan flesh. He was blond all over, with a golden happy trail leading into a trimmed thatch where his cock hung low and heavy. Nate couldn't wait to get his hands all over Cooper and explore every inch of him, even though he was still fuzzy-headed from what had to be the best blow job of his life, and not even remotely capable of getting it up any time soon.

He might have stood there staring all day, but Cooper ran a hand over his own cheek and grimaced. "I'll be right back." He headed into what Nate assumed was the bathroom. The sound of running water a moment later confirmed it for him. When Cooper emerged, his face had been washed and his hair was damp and slicked back. Something in Nate mourned the loss of his visible claim on Cooper—which was crazy, because he'd never been into that sort of caveman shit—but there it was. After knowing him for less than an hour, Nate wanted to mark Cooper for his own.

Fuck, that blow job *had* scrambled his brain.

A droplet of water slid down the side of Cooper's throat and landed in the dip of his collarbone. Nate reached out without thinking and skimmed his thumb across the spot. Cooper's gaze grew dark and heavy, and his voice was a low rumble. "Baby, I'd really like to take you to bed and wreck you right now."

Nate opened his mouth to say he didn't think he'd be up for anything for at least an hour, but instead found himself saying, "I wouldn't mind."

*What the fuck, brain?*

"You know, this isn't what I had planned," Cooper said, stepping closer and settling his broad hands on Nate's hips. "My plan involved a couple of cocktails, maybe a dinner date while I tried to convince you to give me a chance, and then I'd ease you into the whole companion role, because I know you're new to this. But that all went out of the window the minute I saw you. You're" — his breath caught — "fucking irresistible, did you know that?"

Nate's ego swelled at around the same rate as his now-very-interested cock. "Irresistible, huh?" He draped his hands around Cooper's shoulders, and he could feel the heat radiating off him. Werewolves always ran hot, he remembered — in every sense of the word, it seemed. "What is it that does it for you? The gentle aroma of sunscreen and brick dust?"

"Honestly? I have no fucking idea what it is. I just know I want you." Cooper reached up and cupped his chin. Nate found himself trapped under the weight of Cooper's gaze. "The wolf doesn't come out for just anyone, Nate. That was the best sex I've had in years."

Nate ducked his head, unsure what to do with the praise. "It was just a blow job."

"It wasn't *just* anything, baby." Cooper pressed a kiss to his temple. "So when I say you're irresistible, how about you just believe me?"

Nate had no idea what to say to that, and it turned out he didn't need to say anything at all, because Cooper was cupping his face, tilting it and kissing him.

Nate's lips parted in shock and Cooper took full advantage of the fact, pressing his tongue inside and licking into his mouth like he was trying to catch the taste of his own spunk. It was stupid amounts of hot, and Nate decided to just go with it. He kissed Cooper back, letting himself soak up the sexual tension that crackled between them. Before he knew it, his cock was hard again, rubbing against Cooper's own erection—a tease and a promise all at once.

Cooper slid a hand between them and wrapped it around both their lengths. Nate arched up into the heat of his touch, and he could feel the curve of Cooper's smile against his mouth. Cooper pulled back and whispered against the shell of Nate's ear, his breath warm, "Wanna move this to the bedroom, sweet thing? Or you want me to jerk you off nice and slow right here?"

Nate panted and rutted into his hand, unable to decide let alone form words.

"I need an answer, baby." Cooper took his hand away and Nate missed his touch almost at once.

Nate was unsure why, but thinking, let alone talking, was almost impossible, all his cognitive functions buried under a wave of desperation. Right now, his focus was on getting more of Cooper's hands on him, and getting Cooper over him, *in* him. He kissed Cooper again, messy and urgent, and when they parted, he panted out, "Bed?"

Cooper's smile could have lit up Optus Stadium. "I was hoping you'd say that." He leaned in and murmured in Nate's ear, "Gonna let me carry you there?"

Nate's mouth went dry. It was like Cooper could read his thoughts—he'd always wanted to know how it felt for someone to manhandle him. He nodded, and before he knew it, Cooper had his hands under his thighs and was lifting him off his feet. Nate threw his arms around Cooper's wide shoulders and held on. His cock rubbed against Cooper's abs as he strode across the suite towards the bedroom door while holding Nate up like he weighed nothing. Nate didn't hold back the moan that was trying to escape him, because this was the single hottest thing that had happened to him in his *life.*

Cooper huffed out a laugh against the curve of his throat. "You got a thing for werewolf strength, baby?"

"Got a thing for *you*," Nate rasped out, shocked to realise it was true. He was weak for Cooper, had been since the moment he'd heard his voice.

Cooper stopped beside the bed and lowered him onto his back, on whisper-soft sheets that probably cost more than Nate made in a month. He settled himself over Nate, balancing on his elbows, and leaned in and kissed him again, hot and dirty, the movement causing their dicks to brush against each other in a sensual tease. Nate whimpered against Cooper's mouth, heat crackling through his cock and balls, and lightning racing through him at the touch. Cooper hummed and rolled his hips, causing a delicious slide of skin on skin, and, in a voice that could have been bottled and sold as an aphrodisiac, asked, "You gonna let me have all of you, baby?"

"*Yessss*," Nate hissed out, arching his back and chasing more friction. "Please, yes."

Cooper let out a low, almost feral noise of want. Nate found himself lifted and flipped over so he was sprawled on his belly with Cooper pressed against his back, his cock nudging at Nate's arse. Cooper tangled one hand in Nate's hair and tugged, and Nate arched his spine in response and turned his head, exposing his throat. "Beautiful," Cooper growled. His mouth was hot against Nate's skin as he sucked on the tender flesh then ran up the side of his neck. Nate's nerves tingled from head to toe and he rocked his hips, rolling his cock against the bedding as he chased more of the sensation.

"Oh no, baby." Cooper pulled back from where he was kissing Nate's neck, and pressed his hand into the small of Nate's back, pinning him in place. "I'm in charge here. You get to come when I say, and not before. And I say you don't come until I'm inside you."

"Well, get inside me, then," Nate panted, wondering when, exactly, the idea of someone controlling his orgasms had gotten so fucking hot.

Cooper's low chuckle was filthy and delicious. "Oh, I will. Just gotta get you nice and open for me first."

Nate let out a groan and squirmed, spreading his legs wider in blatant invitation. "Do it."

Cooper ran both hands over the globes of his arse, massaging and spreading his cheeks, before Nate felt the press of lips and the scratch of stubble on the curve of his lower back. Cooper's weight lifted off the bed for a moment, but he was back before Nate had a chance to miss him. Then there was the familiar click of a lube cap and slick fingers were gliding down Nate's crease and circling his hole, making the nerve endings there sing. Cooper pressed against his opening, teasing, the pressure increasing with every touch until, at last, he sank one finger deep inside.

Nate arched his back and moaned, because fuck if that didn't feel good. Cooper let out a groan of his own and started up a steady rhythm, pressing in and out, tugging gently at Nate's rim until it was soft and stretched. He added a second finger, twisting his hand, loosening Nate up further before crooking his fingertips *just* right.

When he touched Nate's prostate, Nate let out a shout as pleasure raced through him like he'd touched a live wire.

Cooper made a pleased sound. "Yeah? You like that?"

"Uh-huh," Nate managed, his whole body alight.

"Good." Cooper's voice was thick with dark satisfaction. He continued to finger Nate, brushing against his prostate until Nate was half mad with the need to come—which wasn't going to happen yet, he remembered. Not until Cooper fucked and filled him.

"Please?" Nate whimpered, and he knew he sounded desperate, but right now he didn't care. He just needed Cooper inside him.

"Yeah? You ready to take me, sweetheart?" Cooper drawled, sliding his fingers in and out one last time before withdrawing, leaving Nate empty and aching.

"Uh-huh." Nate rocked against the bed, all his words gone.

Cooper put his hands under Nate's hips and hauled him up and back so that he was balanced on his knees, then ran a hand down his spine, applying gentle pressure until it was arched just so. Nate started stroking himself in long, slow movements, letting out a groan of relief at getting a hand on his cock. He was distracted enough that he took no notice of the crinkle of foil from behind him.

Then Cooper's fingers were back in his arse, spreading him wide and adding more lube before they were replaced by the blunt head of Cooper's cock. As Cooper pressed forward, Nate rocked back, revelling in the fullness when Cooper breached his hole and slid in deep in a single, smooth thrust.

Nate let out a groan as his body adjusted to being filled and stretched, and Cooper echoed it while grinding forward, as if to make sure Nate felt every fat inch of his dick. Then he wrapped his broad hands around Nate's waist, holding him steady. "Ready, baby?"

Without waiting for a reply, Cooper began fucking him in earnest, snapping his hips forward in a fast, desperate rhythm, and the room was filled with the slap of skin on skin. Nate jerked himself off in time to the thrusts, letting out sounds he hadn't even known he could make. Between Cooper hitting his prostate and his own urgent strokes, it didn't take long until he was shaking with the need to come.

Cooper's grip on him tightened and he hauled Nate backward and up onto his knees. He slammed up into him, pulling Nate down onto his cock with a low, animalistic grunt. He fucked up hard enough that Nate's breath left him as Cooper sank even deeper inside him, like he was determined to carve out a space for himself. Cooper's entire body tensed and he hissed as he filled the condom, before reaching around and tugging on Nate's piercing, the sting sharp and sweet and perfect.

Combined with the manhandling that was just the right side of too rough, it was enough to trigger Nate's orgasm. Before he knew it, he was coming like a freight train, his ass clenching down on Cooper's length as Nate shot his release across the bed.

Cooper let out a low growl and ground in deep. Nate had thought he was done, but Cooper's movements must have hit just right because Nate's balls throbbed, and he was shocked to find himself coming again. It seemed to last forever. By the time his cock gave one final twitch, he was exhausted. He sighed and sagged back against Cooper's chest—a sweaty, fucked-out, satisfied heap.

Cooper ran a hand down Nate's ribs and settled it on his stomach, resting his head on Nate's shoulder. "Fucking hell, Nate," he murmured, "that was incredible."

Nate was still drifting on his post-orgasmic high, Cooper's body warm against his back, and all he could do was hum in agreement. He settled his hand over Cooper's, linking their fingers over his stomach. He could feel the hint of a bulge, and knew it was Cooper's cock still buried deep inside him.

It shouldn't have been arousing, but Nate knew he'd be jerking off to the memory of this for the rest of his natural life.

As if reading his thoughts, Cooper whispered, "You like it when I'm all the way in you, huh, baby?" He pressed down and Nate groaned at the pressure, squirming where he was still impaled on Cooper's cock.

"Damn, Nate. You keep moving like that and I'll think you want me to fuck you again."

Nate's ass clenched around Cooper's length like it was *on board* with the idea, and Nate actually considered it for all of three seconds, because Cooper fucking him had felt goddam amazing. But then Cooper trailed his hand down and cupped Nate's limp cock and Nate gasped, oversensitive, dismissing the idea of anything else happening involving his junk—at least until he'd recovered.

"I wish I could," he rasped out, "but I'm only human."

"Yeah, baby, I know." Cooper lowered them to their sides and pulled out. Nate's hole ached in a way that told him he'd been well and truly fucked. "Tell you what," Cooper purred in his ear. "You rest, and maybe when you wake up, we'll do it all again. And after that I'll take you somewhere nice for that getting-to-know-you dinner, yeah?"

Nate could feel the pull of sleep, despite it being early afternoon, but his lips still curved into a lazy smile at the idea that Cooper wanted to take him out. "Pretty sure you know me inside and out," he said, stifling a yawn.

Cooper huffed out a laugh against the nape of his neck. "Smartarse."

"Oh, did I not list that in my profile? My mistake." Nate grinned, right before another yawn forced its way out.

Cooper sat up and got out of bed, pulling the quilt up over Nate's shoulders. Nate intended to stay awake and wait for him to come back, but after two mind-blowing orgasms, the lure of sleep was too great.

He wasn't sure how long he slept for, but he woke to the sound of Cooper's voice in the other room. He lay there, ears straining to pick up the conversation, but he could only hear one voice, so he guessed it must be a phone call.

"I don't care," Cooper said. "They've been warned before."

There was silence before Cooper said, voice raised, "No. I want them terminated, and all evidence that they were ever there removed."

*What the fuck?*

"Yes, I'm sure. And, Jonas? Make sure word gets out. Some people seem to have forgotten that when it comes to my business, I don't play around. This might remind them." Cooper's voice was hard, and it made Nate's gut twist with something that wasn't quite fear, but was a close cousin.

"One more thing. You know I'm on Companion time, so unless somebody dies or the place goes up in flames, I don't want to know."

Silence, then Cooper lowered his voice and said, "Let's just say he fell into my lap, and leave it at that. I have to go, Jonas. He's awake."

Right, because freaky werewolf senses.

Nate sat up in bed, his mind whirling. What the hell was it that Cooper did that he was having people...terminated?

Obviously he was rich if he could afford the amount he was paying for Nate's company. And terminated was just a fancy word for giving someone the sack, right? Still, Nate couldn't help but be reminded of every mafia movie he'd ever seen.

He shook his head at his own ridiculousness.

Cooper wasn't a criminal, or he never would have been allowed in the Programme to begin with.

Still.

*"He fell into my lap."*

The computer glitch that had resulted in Nate being here. The way Liz had fallen all over herself to get Nate to meet him. Maybe Cooper did something boring, like cardboard box manufacture, but maybe he was tied up in...what, exactly, Nate wasn't sure, but he did know that the underworld boasted a high proportion of werewolves. It was a simple fact that super strength and a killer instinct were attributes that lent themselves to the thug life.

The bedroom door swung open, and Cooper came in wearing a hotel robe. He was smiling, and Nate was distracted from his thoughts by how fucking pretty he was.

"Hey, baby," Cooper said, stripping out of his robe and diving onto the bed. He wrapped his arms around

Nate and rolled them so Nate was on top. "Ready for round two?" he asked, his eyes dark with want. He tangled his hand in Nate's hair and pulled him in for a kiss. By the time he'd finished exploring Nate's mouth, Nate was on board.

Cooper spent the next hour doing what he'd said he would — wrecking Nate thoroughly. He fucked into him with long languid strokes, rolling his hips in a way that should have been illegal, and by the time they were done, Nate was so fuck-drunk that any questions he'd had about who Cooper Hudson might be had flown right out of his head.

# Chapter Four

When Nate turned from the mirror and spread his arms, saying, "How do I look?" it took all of Cooper's self-control not to bend him over the dining table, yank his suit pants down and fuck him right there. It wasn't that Nate was wearing anything all that special to dinner, although the sight of white shirtsleeves cuffed against tan skin and the movements of his muscled forearms did have Cooper's cock twitching.

It was more the knowledge that underneath that crisp white shirt, he was sporting a couple of lovebites from earlier in the day that marked him as Cooper's. When combined with that surprising nipple piercing and his inked skin, well. Cooper hadn't been lying when he'd told Nate he was irresistible. He was already mourning the end of their week together.

But he couldn't step away from his job for any longer than that, not if he wanted to keep things running smoothly. He'd already had to fire one of his newer employees today when the man had been caught sharing screenshots of information for the second time.

Cooper wasn't about to tolerate that, not in a business where discretion was everything.

"Is something wrong?" Cooper was pulled out of his thoughts when Nate paused with his hands on his belt buckle. "Is this not swanky enough? Because I hate to break it to you, but this is as good as it gets on my wage." A furrow appeared in his forehead under the lock of hair that insisted on falling forward.

Cooper stepped towards him and brushed the hair back. "Actually, I was thinking how very fuckable you looked."

Nate flushed. "Flatterer."

"It's not flattery. It's the truth. I'd be happy to skip dinner, bend you over the table and take you right now." Even as he said it, Cooper was almost tempted, and wondered how Nate would feel about room service.

Nate shook his head. "Don't even think about it. You promised me seafood."

"I did, didn't I? And I'm a man of my word." Cooper ran his fingers through Nate's fringe once more. He couldn't help the way his voice dropped lower as he traced a thumb over Nate's lower lip. "But maybe later?"

"*Definitely* later," Nate agreed with a grin.

Cooper let out a pleased rumble at the thought.

Nate placed a hand on his chest, right over the centre of the vibrations, and he sounded more amazed than afraid when he said, "Fuck, listen to that. You're all animal under there, aren't you?"

"Only for you, sweetheart." It was true. When in human company, Cooper kept his animal side locked down *hard*—some people were still cautious even a decade after the werewolf reveal, and he'd seen one too many YouTube videos of someone claiming they'd been 'threatened' by the merest hint of a fang — and he had no problem staying in control.

With Nate, though? It was like his wolf was circling just below the surface ready to break free at any moment, and Cooper wanted to *let* it. He'd never experienced anything like it, and it was disconcerting and exhilarating all at once.

He leaned in, pressed his face to the curve of Nate's neck and inhaled. There was a spicy undercurrent to Nate's normal aroma, one that Cooper was quick to identify as lust. "Are you *sure* we can't get room service?" Cooper mumbled against his throat, teasing.

Nate stiffened, hands clutching at his sides, and bitterness flooded his scent. "Sure."

Cooper snapped his head up. "What's wrong?"

Nate ducked his head, avoiding Cooper's gaze. "Nothing. It's fine." His heartbeat thundered at the lie.

Cooper used two fingers to lift his chin. "Don't lie to me, Nate. I can hear it."

Nate muttered something that sounded suspiciously like "*fucking werewolf senses*" before swallowing. "It's — I got dressed for dinner and it was a waste of time, that's all."

Cooper's brow wrinkled in confusion. "Why was it a waste of time?"

Nate gave him a disbelieving look. "Because you *just* said we're staying in."

"I was *teasing*. You look so delicious that I want to stay here and do lots of filthy things to you, sure, but I didn't mean we were *actually* skipping our date."

Nate relaxed, but only just. "Oh. I, um." He swallowed again. "Oh." He gave a hesitant smile, and the burnt coffee smell of his anxiety lessened.

Cooper was still confused. "Nate, why did you agree to staying in if you didn't want to?"

Nate shrugged. "I mean. You call the shots, right? Since you're the one paying."

Cooper's stomach dropped. *Fuck.* "Nate, no. It's not—" He let out a groan and tipped his head back, wondering what he'd done that had made Nate assume he was the kind of entitled wanker who'd change plans just because he wanted to get his dick wet. "Nate," he tried again. "It's not like that."

"Pretty sure it's just like that," Nate said. "You pay, we play."

Cooper ran a hand down his face and wondered how he'd fucked up so badly. "*I'm* not like that," he said. "We might have entered into a contract, but that doesn't mean I call all the shots. I don't intend to spend the next week with you chained to the bed." He put a hand on Nate's shoulder and placed a soft kiss on his cheek, desperate to reassure him.

There was a moment's silence, then Nate snorted, his scent returning to its normal base notes of sea breeze and vanilla. "Nah, mate. Chains are extra."

Cooper barked out a startled laugh, and his gut uncoiled as the tension between them eased. "No chains, noted," he said, then cupped Nate's face in his hands and kissed him again, just to make himself feel better.

Nate let out a breathy sigh against his lips, one hand making its way to the back of Cooper's head and messing up his hairstyle, but Cooper didn't give a fuck right now, not when Nate was kissing him back with such eagerness.

It took all of Cooper's self-control to end the kiss, but he managed it. He took a second to clear his head and pulled his phone out, fingers flying, because if he didn't get them out of here right now, there was no guarantee they'd make their reservation. "Uber's on its way," he said, his breathing rapid. "Six minutes."

Nate nodded, wearing a dazed expression. "Right. Dinner." He traced a fingertip over his bottom lip, and it was distracting as fuck. Cooper wondered if six minutes was long enough to back Nate into a wall, drop to his knees and blow him.

Just as he took a step forward to test the theory, Nate held up a hand. "Whatever you're thinking of doing, save it for later."

"Who says I was thinking of doing anything?" Cooper protested, hands spread wide to show his innocence.

Nate smirked, looking far too pleased with himself. "Coop, your eyes were glowing."

Cooper's jaw dropped. "No, they weren't."

Nate held up his thumb and forefinger in a pinch. "Little bit, mate."

Well, shit. It wasn't the first time Cooper's eyes had glowed gold when he was aroused, but the last time it had happened, he'd been a pup of sixteen, just discovering what his dick was for, and still learning to keep them both — the pup *and* the dick — under control. He did his best to change the subject. "Oh, so it's Coop now, huh?"

"It suits you," Nate said. "It's all, like, rakish and debonair and shit. And it's sexy as fuck — like you."

"Well, in that case," Cooper said, "I like it."

Nate's smirk grew into a full-blown smile, all teeth and gorgeousness, and Cooper felt a warm glow in his chest at the fact that it was directed at him.

His phone buzzed in his hand and after he'd read the message, he held the phone up. "Our driver, Ahmed, will meet us in three minutes."

"See? You wouldn't have had time for what you were planning." Nate quirked an eyebrow. "What were you gonna do, anyway?"

"Oh," Cooper said, low and sultry, "I was just going to blow you, that's all. Back you up against that wall, fish your dick out and get it all spit-slick and sloppy, then let you slide it right down my throat nice and easy, choke me on that thick fucking thing." He turned towards the door, congratulating himself on the wave of lust that rolled off Nate, and called over his shoulder, "But like you said, no time. Shame. Shall we go?"

Nate's breathing hitched, and he *whined* as he followed Cooper to the door. "Fucking *hell*, Coop. That's just cruel."

Cooper gave him a bright smile. "Oh, I don't know. I mean, there's always later, right? And now I get to spend the entire evening watching you squirm in anticipation, and *you* get a phenomenal blow job after dinner."

The look Nate gave him was nothing short of scorching. Desire stirred deep in Cooper's belly. "Fuck yeah, I do. And since you say you're *not* calling all the shots, I'm telling you now, we're not staying for dessert."

"Of course not," Cooper said. He stood aside to let Nate exit, then squeezed his arse as he passed, adding, "The sweetest thing on the menu tonight is you, baby."

\* \* \* \*

Teasing Nate had been a tactical error, because Cooper hadn't accounted for one possibility — that Nate would tease him back.

His libido was already in overdrive at the mental picture of Nate with his pants around his knees begging for Cooper to suck his dick, and Nate didn't help matters, tilting his head back and sliding fresh oysters from their shell into his open mouth, following them with throaty moans that *had* to be deliberate.

Cooper's wolf whined. It took all his control to stay seated and not drag Nate off to the restrooms and fuck his throat. He had to force himself to fix his gaze on his plate after Nate licked a dribble of oyster juice from the corner of his mouth, his eyes sparkling with amusement. "Nothing like a fresh, salty mouthful." He grinned.

Cooper arched an eyebrow. "You're really going to tease me right now?"

Nate's smile widened. "You started it, Coop."

"I may have underestimated you," Cooper admitted, grinning back. This might be torture, but it was the fun kind. Given the choice between a laughing, irreverent Nate and the subdued, uncertain Nate from earlier who'd been willing to forgo dinner on Cooper's say-so and who had assumed he was nothing more than a fucktoy, this version was far preferable.

The waiter cleared their starter plates and brought their meals, and Cooper did his best to remind himself that as fuckable as Nate was, there was more to him than that. "Why work as a labourer?" he asked. "Was it something you wanted to do?"

Nate shrugged. "Mum and Dad split up when I was seventeen. Dad moved to Queensland, and Mum moved us in with her new bloke. It kind of threw off my year twelve exams, and I was never going to uni anyway, so I started looking for a job. I've always liked being outside, and a mate knew a guy, so I did a two-week work trial, didn't fuck up and Sully hired me. The end."

"And you've never considered an apprenticeship to qualify? You seem smart enough."

Nate shook his head. "Nah, who'd be a boss? I like having no responsibilities. Sully's a good bloke to work for." He tilted his head and observed Cooper for a second before asking, "What about you? You never said what you do, but I can tell you're all kinds of important. What is it, banking or something?"

Cooper blinked, unprepared for the question. "Or something. Corporate bullshit. Nothing exciting." He waved a hand in a vague motion while he cast about for a way to change the subject. "What do your parents think about you working as a companion?"

"What do yours think of you hiring one?" Nate shot back.

Cooper gave a rueful smile. "Fair point."

"I'm not a kid, Coop. I know what I signed up for. And so far? It's pretty good. Although" — he licked his lips — "I do wish the hot guy I'm with would hurry up and eat his lobster. And then we could go back to the hotel, and he could eat my arse."

It was just unfortunate that his comment fell into one of those perfect, unplanned silences that happen in public spaces, and echoed around the restaurant.

Someone tittered at the next table. Someone else cleared their throat. Cooper had to shove a chunk of lobster into his mouth to stifle a laugh when Nate muttered, "Well, fuck," and flushed deep red under his tan.

"Does that come before or after the arse-eating?"

Nate groaned, rubbing his hands down his face, before he huffed out a laugh and shook his head, face still flaming.

He picked up his beer and took a long swig. As he watched Nate's throat work, Cooper's amusement faded and was replaced with a hot stab of lust, his low-simmering arousal flaring into something more urgent. "Eat your dinner, baby," he said, his voice an urgent growl.

Nate's eyes widened and his lips parted, the scent of *wantneedyes* rolling off him. His throat clicked as he swallowed and he gave a nod. "Yes, sir."

And 'sir' wasn't even Cooper's kink, but fuck if it didn't have his cock straining enough that he wondered how he was going to walk out of the place.

He debated dragging Nate away there and then, before recalling their earlier misunderstanding. No. He was an adult. He could keep his shit together at least long enough to finish dinner and prove to Nate that he wasn't some pushy, entitled dick.

His wolf whined its disapproval.

Cooper told it to shut the fuck up.

It was obvious he wasn't the only one no longer interested in dinner, though, because Nate managed two-thirds of his meal before pushing his plate away. "I'm done."

Cooper pushed his chair back. "Same." He stood, thankful his erection had subsided somewhat, and went to pay the bill, Nate following hot on his heels.

He ordered their ride and as they waited outside, he draped one arm around Nate's shoulders and drew him close, whispering, "I should warn you, baby. I intend to pay you back for teasing me earlier. I'm going to fuck you till you beg."

Nate leaned into the touch and murmured back, "See, you say that, but from the look on your face, I'm guessing you'll blow your load in about seven seconds once you're inside my arse."

Cooper pulled back and crossed his arms across his chest in a show of being offended. "Rude! I'll last at least ten. Maybe fifteen, if you're lucky."

Nate burst out laughing, and Cooper let him think he was joking — but if he was honest, he was so pent up that seven seconds seemed about accurate. The one compensation was that as a shifter, he'd be raring to go in five minutes.

And in another five after that. Perks of werewolf biology.

"What are you grinning about?" Nate nudged him with an elbow.

"Oh, I was just thinking about the filthy things I'm going to do to you."

"With me."

Cooper's brow furrowed. "Pardon?"

Nate let out a breath. "I don't want you doing anything *to* me."

Cooper froze in place, his chest tightening. Was Nate pulling out of their contract?

Before he had a chance to panic, Nate leaned in and pressed a quick kiss to his cheek. "To be clear, I still want you to fuck me stupid. But before, you said it's not like that. *You're* not like that. So, um, I want you to do all sorts of filthy things, but I want you to do them *with* me. There's a difference."

The band around Cooper's chest loosened, and he drew in a deep breath, nuzzling the side of Nate's throat and inhaling the *vanilla-ocean-fuckme* scent he was fast becoming addicted to. "Baby," he murmured into the soft skin, "I'm gonna do *so* many fun things — *with* you." He licked a stripe up Nate's neck to make his point. Nate's pupils went dark and his breathing hitched, cheeks staining pink.

Cooper didn't think he could hold back for much longer, and he thanked any gods that were listening when their Uber driver chose that moment to arrive.

They piled into the car, and he noted the rosary beads hanging from the rear vision mirror. Nate must have spotted them too, because they sat in the back seat without touching, a picture of innocence, for the three-minute ride to the hotel.

They tumbled out of the car and into the hotel and an empty elevator. Cooper took advantage of the privacy to slide a hand inside the back of Nate's dress pants and squeeze his arse, earning a soft groan that went straight to his cock. Once they got to their room, Cooper didn't waste any time backing Nate against the door as soon as he'd slammed it shut, pressing his tongue against the seam of his lips, hungry and desperate.

Nate moaned into the kiss and a warm note, like cinnamon and honey, permeated his scent — a sure sign that he was enjoying this, if the enthusiasm with which he was licking into Cooper's mouth wasn't enough of a clue. Cooper ground forward, a fresh burst of arousal racing up his spine in a long line of heat, and he remembered his earlier promise. He stopped kissing Nate just so that he could growl low in his ear. "Want me to suck your dick, baby?"

Nate drew a stuttery breath. "First I want you to fuck me — bare."

Cooper growled, heat pooling in his belly at the thought of being inside Nate, nothing between them, and feeling the heat and clutch of him around his dick. "You—you'd let me?" His voice was barely a whisper.

Nate nodded. "I assume you had to go through the same medical I did, yeah?"

Cooper nodded, unable to speak around the lump in his throat. Blood thundered in his ears and his cock pressed against his zipper, a solid heat.

"Then let's ditch the condoms," Nate said. "Because I've always wanted to try it, and I might never get another chance with a guaranteed safe bet."

Cooper pushed down the sharp stab of jealousy that reared its head at the thought of Nate sleeping with anyone else, ever. Nate was offering him something special, and Cooper was going to grab hold of it with both hands. "Fuck, yes."

Cooper grasped Nate around the waist and lifted him into the air, high enough that when he leaned forward, he could fasten his mouth over the fabric of Nate's shirt and tease at his piercing. Nate gave a startled laugh, but soon enough it transformed into a series of breathy whimpers as Cooper sucked and nipped and mouthed, his cock throbbing at every sound Nate made. There was a damp patch on Nate's shirt, and his nipple was a hard nub beneath Cooper's teeth and tongue.

It was exhilarating, and it wasn't anywhere near enough.

Cooper was half-drunk on Nate's scent and presence, addicted to him in a way he'd never experienced, and with the vision of his naked cock sliding into Nate's plush insides taunting him, Cooper couldn't wait any longer. He spun and walked them through to the bedroom, Nate wrapped around him. He set Nate on his feet next to the bed and stripped down while Nate hurried to do the same.

The curtains were still open, the lights of the city twinkling in the darkness, gleaming as they reflected off the blackness of the Swan River. As pretty as the view was, it paled in comparison next to the sight of Nate, naked and eager, grabbing the lube from the bedside table and settling himself on his back. His arse was set at the edge of the bed and his legs were parted in silent invitation, heels pressing into the mattress and leaving him wide open for the taking. He squirted lube into his palm and worked his cock for a brief moment before snaking his hand down between his legs and pressing against his hole, letting out a filthy groan as his fingertip sank inside.

"Jesus *fuck*, Nate." Cooper stared, mesmerised.

Nate grinned, eyes bright and colour high in his cheeks, and tilted his hips up. The new angle had his finger sliding deeper, and he gave a low grunt before he rasped out, "Want you to fuck me like this."

Cooper's heartbeat thundered in his ears and he didn't waste any time, striding across the room. He stepped into the welcoming space between Nate's legs, squirted lube on his fingers and replaced Nate's hand with his own. When he plunged two fingers inside, Nate gave a filthy moan. It was a sound that Cooper wanted to hear more of.

Nate was still soft and open from earlier so Cooper didn't spend long fingering him, not with Nate throwing his head back every time Cooper grazed his prostate. Nate moaned, and gasped out, "Just fucking *do* it, Coop."

Cooper slicked up his cock and pressed the head against Nate's opening, the tip sinking in with almost no resistance, and *fuck*.

"Oh fuck, yeah, Coop. Fuck me." Nate panted, eyes dark with desire, hooking his hands behind his thighs and holding himself open in invitation.

Cooper pushed inside, gripping Nate's knees as an anchor and sinking all the way into the tight heat before stilling, overwhelmed, because fucking Nate with a condom had been amazing, but experiencing the hot clutch of his arse with nothing between them? Feeling the silky soft caress of his insides as Cooper fucked into him and carved out a space for himself?

*Phenomenal.*

Cooper's fangs burst through his gums, his vision flared and his wolf took over. His breath came in short snarls as he rutted forward, Nate writhing and moaning and clenching around his length, and he managed a bare handful of thrusts before his balls drew up tight and he knew he had no hope of making this last.

He grasped Nate around the waist and dragged him back onto his cock while Nate wrapped a hand around his own erection and stripped it furiously, chanting, *"Fuck, fuck, fuck,"* under his breath as he arched his back and tilted his hips up.

Cooper sank deeper into that glorious, welcoming heat. The tension in his spine crackled, his heart raced and every nerve in his body sang, seeking release. He growled, low and urgent, and snapped his hips in a series of fast, savage strokes that made Nate cry out with a desperation that Cooper shared.

Nate tensed around him, and seconds later he came all over his stomach and hand in a flood, his arse clutching at Cooper's length. That, combined with the way he went limp in Cooper's hold while still impaled on his cock, was enough to have Cooper burying himself deep one last time before heat raced through his veins. His cock throbbed and pulsed, and he came with a grunt as pleasure overwhelmed him. Nate's hole spasmed around him, milking him of his release, and Cooper rocked his hips forward, making it last as long as he could.

When it was over, Cooper stood there panting, happy to be planted deep inside Nate, staking his claim. He would have stayed there, except his legs didn't seem to want to hold him up.

He eased his softening cock out of Nate's arse, a wave of possessiveness washing over him at the sight of his cum dripping down Nate's thighs, leaving glistening streaks that marked his claim.

"Fucking hell, Coop," Nate rasped, "I don't think I have a bone left in my body." He let out a contented sigh, his heels sliding off the bed and leaving him spread wide, covered in jizz and a light sheen of sweat. He was filthy and irresistible, and Cooper's wolf, which had retreated, rumbled in contentment at the sight of his sated mate.

*Wait.*

*What?*

Cooper staggered back a step before managing to catch himself and sit on the side of the bed, his mind racing.

*Mate?*

Werewolf mates were a thing, but it was about a fifty-fifty split as to who had one, and Cooper had never suspected he'd find his. And he *definitely* hadn't expected it to be the man he'd hired for a week of summer sex, on the understanding that when this was over, he'd pay him and they'd part ways.

Well, *fuck*. This was going to be fun to explain.

"Coop? You okay?" Nate rolled over and shuffled up the bed, propping himself up on one elbow, his brow creased. "Is it—was the no condom thing too weird?"

Cooper swallowed around the lump in his throat. "No."

"Then what is it? Because I gotta say, all my childhood Sunday school guilt is coming into play here and I feel like I fucked up somehow, so if you could tell me that's not the case, that'd be great."

Cooper closed his eyes and took a deep, calming breath, all the while wondering what the fuck to say.

*Guess who has two thumbs and a true mate?*

*How do you feel about relocating to Sydney?*

*So, funny story. You know you asked about my job? I'm the CEO of SCP. Also, you're my mate. Crazy, right?*

"Coop? The guilt is intensifying."

When Cooper opened his eyes, Nate was sitting cross-legged on the bed and biting his bottom lip. His fingers were tapping out a staccato pattern against his thigh and he looked about four seconds from losing his shit.

No.

Cooper couldn't drop this on him, not after knowing him for just a day.

He had the rest of the week. He'd figure out some way to break it to Nate, and it would be fine.

Probably.

He reached out and pressed a palm on top of Nate's hand, stilling his movements. "You were perfect, baby," he said, and that, at least, wasn't a lie. "I was just lightheaded there for a minute." He gave a smile that he hoped looked genuine. "I think you broke me, and now I need to pass out."

Nate chewed on a fingernail. "Honestly? I think I broke *me* as well, because fuck, that was intense, and passing out sounds amazing. Is it a werewolf thing, or because we went bareback?"

Cooper swallowed. "Yeah. A werewolf thing. We go wild for skin on skin."

It wasn't quite a lie.

It just wasn't quite the truth.

# Chapter Five

Nate woke up at five because he always woke up at five. Just because he was spending the week with one of the hottest men he'd ever met, that didn't mean his body clock wasn't still a dick.

Truth be told, though, he found he didn't mind being awake. They'd both passed out last night, with Cooper holding him tight enough that Nate's back had been slick with sweat despite the air-con blasting, but Nate had been so wiped out that after a few desultory shoves that had no effect, he'd fallen asleep in spite of the heat and closeness.

At some time during the night, they must have moved apart, because the doona had been thrown on the floor and Cooper was now sprawled on his back, an arm above his head and one knee crooked to the side. Since he was still fast asleep, Nate propped himself up on one elbow and took the opportunity to ogle him shamelessly.

He hadn't had the chance before, because it seemed like every time they got naked they were both already desperate. Which. Nate liked sex. Loved it, even. But something about Cooper made him *crave* it, in a way that was both foreign and thrilling.

Shit. Maybe he had a werewolf kink.

He grinned to himself. Perhaps that meant he could do the SCP again next year, or even, once his time with Cooper was done, put himself back in the selection pool and find another wolf for the rest of the month.

His stomach lurched without warning, and a sour taste flooded his mouth. He wrinkled his nose, wondering if he'd eaten a bad prawn, before dismissing the idea — he would have been a lot sicker a lot faster if that were the case.

He trailed a fingertip over Cooper's firm chest, drawing trails in the dark hair sprinkled with silver, and something about the motion, combined with the heat of Cooper's skin, soothed him and made the bad taste in his mouth dissipate.

Cooper was drop-dead gorgeous. His skin was flawless — because *werewolves* didn't get scars when they fell off their bike and split their knees open in Year Three — and he was the perfect ratio of height to muscle. Nate wondered if he worked out, before remembering that werewolves didn't *have* to work out. The same genes that gave them the ability to control their shift could be employed to tweak their everyday appearance, which was why all werewolves were hotter than fuck.

Nate was the slightest bit jealous, if he were honest — he would have given anything at thirteen to be able to manipulate his teeth into a straight line instead of wearing braces for a year.

Coop had nice teeth. He had *great* teeth.

He had great…everything.

Nate stroked Cooper's skin, sliding his hand down towards his stomach and coming to rest on Cooper's abs.

"Morning." Cooper's voice was rough with sleep, the added rasp making it even more intoxicating. His eyelids were half open, and he gave Nate a sleepy smile before he stretched, his muscles bunching under Nate's hand. "You checking out the goods, baby?"

Nate gave a half-shrug. "Busted. But in my defence, you're hot as fuck."

Cooper let out a laugh. He half-rolled so he was facing Nate and reached out and ran a hand through his messy hair. "You're a hell of a pretty sight to wake up to yourself."

Just then, Cooper's phone pinged and he rolled away and grabbed it, giving Nate a great view of his solid thighs and perfect, toned arse. Nate itched with the need to grab it.

Before he had a chance though, Cooper turned back holding his phone and looking far too pleased with himself.

"Good news?" Nate asked, settling himself back against the headboard.

"Just confirmation of today's plans," Cooper said, still grinning like the cat that got the cream.

"I didn't know we had plans?"

"We do now." Cooper paused in the act of standing, a crease furrowing his brow. "You own boardies, right? Never mind. If you don't, we can pick a pair up."

"No, I have a pair." Nate got out of bed as well, curious now. "Why do I need boardies? Are we going to the beach?" He could get behind spending the day eyeing off Cooper in a Speedo.

"Yeah, baby. I thought we'd spend the day at Rottnest."

Nate was sure his own broad smile mirrored Cooper's. "Oh, fuck yeah! I haven't been to Rotto since Year Seven School Camp. We had to leave early because we all got food poisoning—which, let me tell you, twenty puking kids does *not* make for a fun ferry ride."

Cooper laughed. "That sounds bloody awful."

"It was. I think it's why I haven't gone back since. Teenage vomit ferry trauma is a hell of a thing to overcome."

"Lucky we're not taking the ferry, then. We're flying."

Nate's mouth dropped open, but he didn't know why he was surprised. "Of course we're flying. Of course."

Cooper gave a lazy shrug. "It's the fastest way there. I didn't come across the country not to get my quokka selfie. I made some calls yesterday, and I was waiting to hear back. Chopper leaves at ten, and we'll be back for dinner."

"Wait, you mean you didn't pull extra strings and get accommodation as well?" Nate grinned.

Cooper made an exasperated sound. "I tried, but Jesus, Nate, I'm not a miracle worker. It's impossible to find a bed on Rottnest in the middle of summer."

He looked so put out that Nate had to stifle a laugh. Cooper Hudson might be a big shot, but no matter how important he was—and even if he *was* some sort of underworld kingpin—he was *still* no match for the labyrinth that was the Rottnest accommodation booking system.

Nate almost felt sorry for him.

"Don't feel too bad, Coop," Nate said. "A Rotto booking is hot property. People book that shit a year in advance."

Cooper's eyebrows rose. "A year? *Why*?"

"Part of it's because of the beaches and the quokkas, and part of it's in case there's a stray Hemsworth hanging around."

"Stray…you know what? Never mind."

Cooper ran a hand through his messy hair and stood there with one hand on his hip, sleep-rumpled and absolutely mouth-watering.

Nate took a step towards him, intending to get his hands all over that, but the tug and scratch of his stomach hair reminded of the fact they hadn't cleaned up last night, both of them too wiped, and now he was covered in his own dried jizz. He wrinkled his nose and considered. Just because he needed to get clean, that didn't mean he couldn't also *have* some fun. He stepped in close, settling his hands on Cooper's hips. "Wanna join me in the shower?"

Cooper wrapped his arms around Nate, leaning in for a long, slow kiss before pulling back and husking out, "Yeah. Maybe I could give you that blow job."

"Maybe we could trade." Nate let his hands roam over Cooper's sides and back, enjoying the warmth that radiated from the flesh under his fingertips.

Cooper let out a rumble from deep in his chest and kissed Nate again, licking into his mouth. Regardless of morning breath, it was still hotter than sin and made Nate want to drop to his knees right there. Fuck, what was it about Cooper that made a simple kiss so intoxicating?

Maybe Nate *did* have a werewolf kink.

Cooper pulled back and grabbed Nate's hand, dragging him into the bathroom with a determination that had Nate wondering if maybe Cooper felt whatever this was between them too. But he couldn't ask, could he? What would he even say?

*Do you feel like there's a special connection between us?*

*Are you as attracted to me as I am to you?*

*Is this more than just sex?*

Right. Because *that* didn't sound like his head was jammed fair up his own arse.

No, Cooper was just a man with a hell of a sex drive, who knew what he wanted — and what he currently wanted was Nate. Odds were, he'd be this eager whoever his partner was.

Nate wasn't special.

But it was hard to remember that when Cooper draped himself round Nate's back under the rainfall showerhead and washed his stomach and chest in a way that was almost worshipful. His hard cock pressed against the crease of Nate's arse while he nuzzled and nipped along the curve of his neck, and one soapy hand worked Nate's cock until he was right on the edge before Cooper dropped to his knees and sucked him off, a broad palm pressing Nate back against the marble tiles, Cooper humming with satisfaction when Nate came down his throat in half a minute flat.

It was no hardship to return the favour, because not only did Nate get his hands and mouth on Cooper's magnificent cock, but he also got to see Cooper with his head thrown back, his mouth hanging open in silent bliss, his hands clutched in Nate's hair, while he fell apart even faster than Nate had.

When *that* happened, yeah. Nate felt pretty fucking special.

\* \* \* \*

The view from the chopper was breath-taking. The skies were clear, and the ocean sparkled as sunlight danced off the waves, a vista of rippling aquas and blues with white caps dotted about, adding colour and movement. The water varied from almost inky black in some spots to crystalline in others, and there were parts where Nate could see right down to the sandy ocean floor through the sea-green water. Even from this height he spotted a school of fish darting in and out of a great swathe of seaweed that was swaying with the motion of the waves.

When they reached Rottnest, the pilot circled the entire island. Nate got a clear view of all the bays and separate beaches that made up the coast of the popular tourist spot, where figures on pushbikes dotted along the various roads. Rottnest was just as stunning as he remembered, and anticipation bubbled up in his chest. Nate was a beach baby, always had been, and he couldn't wait to feel the cool salt water against his skin. It had been too long since he'd done this.

He turned from the window towards Cooper so he could point out one of the spots that was good for snorkelling, only to find Coop wasn't looking at the island at all, but instead watching Nate, his expression intent. Nate flashed him a smile and Coop blinked once, giving his head a slight shake before smiling, back from wherever he'd been.

When they landed and climbed out of the chopper, the heat of the day hit Nate full force, sweat trickling down his forehead and the back of his neck. It was somewhere in the mid-thirties, scorching hot, but since he wasn't working in it, Nate didn't mind too much. Nothing beat swimming in the ocean when summer was at its peak, and this was ideal beach weather.

Cooper grabbed both their backpacks in one hand and strode off, giving Nate a perfect view of his arse. Cooper had dressed down today in boardies, a singlet and thongs, yet he somehow still managed to look smoking hot. Nate wasn't sure how he managed it. It should be illegal to look that good in board shorts, or for anyone to have calves that were that tan and lickable.

Cooper paused and turned, his raised eyebrow visible over the frames of his sunnies. "Everything all right?"

"Just appreciating the view," Nate called back, slipping his own sunnies on and hurrying to catch up.

The smirk on Cooper's face suggested he knew just which scenery Nate was talking about.

They made their way to the small cluster of shops and cafés at Thompson's Bay that passed for the island settlement, joining the throng of people crowding the bakery and picking up a couple of sports drinks each, both of them laughing at the signs on the shop door prohibiting entry to quokkas.

Then they collected their bikes and snorkelling gear from the rental place, and after consulting a map, headed off across the island towards Parker Point.

Nate led the way. Cooper *said* it was because he'd been here before, but Nate could feel the heat of Cooper's gaze on him as he biked along the pathway.

He suspected Cooper just wanted to appreciate his own view.

He played into it, lifting his arse off the seat and waggling it as he biked up the first hill, and stopping at the crest to put his hand on his hips and arch his back, knowing just what kind of picture he made. Cooper skidded to a stop beside him and let out a low growl. "Are you trying to get me arrested for public indecency?"

Nate grinned. "You're not doing anything indecent, though."

"No, but I will if you keep that up." Cooper reached across and gripped Nate's handlebars, then leaned over and kissed his cheek. "I'm serious. Stop teasing, baby."

Nate rolled his eyes. "Fine. But telling me not to tease is pretty bloody rich, coming from the man whose arse should be illegal in those shorts."

Cooper laughed and rode away.

It was a pleasant enough ride despite the relentless heat, and they didn't rush, stopping along the way to take plenty of photos, but it was still as hot as balls. There were a lot more hills than Nate remembered from when he had been a kid. His singlet was sticking to his back with perspiration by the time they approached the bay, but he perked up when he saw a cluster of small, furry creatures in the shade of the low bushes, right beside the road and in the perfect spot for photos.

"Coop! Quokkas!"

Cooper stopped and dismounted, setting his bike on its stand before walking towards the animals. Nate shadowed him, phone at the ready. As Cooper approached, two quokkas hopped right up to him. He crouched down, and Nate got a halfway decent shot of him next to the animals before he straightened up again.

"Wow, they're fearless little bastards, aren't they?" Cooper said, fascinated.

"Oh yeah. They know they're not in any danger."

Cooper looked almost offended at that. "They might be. I'm an apex predator."

"Uh-huh," Nate said, as a quokka hopped up onto Cooper's foot.

He wasn't prepared when Cooper froze, a low rumble coming from him. When Nate looked from Cooper's foot to his face, Cooper looked almost horrified, and the tips of his fangs were peeking over his bottom lip.

"Coop?"

Cooper closed his eyes, and when he opened them again, they were blazing gold. He glared at the creature, and Nate could have sworn that it gave a grin in response. Cooper swallowed, and through clenched teeth bit out, "Get. It. Off."

Nate raised his eyebrows. "Really? It's tiny." He tilted his head, trying to make sense of Cooper's reaction. "Are you afraid of a fucking *quokka*? Because it's cute as fuck, and you look like you're freaking out."

Cooper's nostrils flared, and his hands clenched into fists at his side. "I'm not—" He exhaled, closed his eyes again and mumbled something too low for Nate to hear.

"Sorry, what?" Nate crouched down and observed the quokka as he tried to figure out what the problem was.

"I said, it's a *threat*."

"No it isn't. You could swallow it whole—but please don't. There are massive fines for that."

Cooper let out a noisy sigh and ran a hand down his face. "Nate, my wolf sees that fat little fuck as a threat to *you*, my companion. It's put itself between us, which means my instincts need it gone. So either you move the fucking thing, or I punt it across the road. But either way, I want it off my foot."

A growl escaped him, and his hands unclenched and clenched.

Nate's jaw dropped. He'd heard that wolves could have a protective streak, but as far as he knew, that only applied to their pack members or mates.

Wait. Did that mean Cooper considered him *pack?*

Nate's mind whirled as he reached out a fingertip and shoved at the creature as he murmured, "Hey, little guy. You wanna move? Because otherwise Cooper's gonna play quokka soccer, and that's a bad time all round."

The quokka blinked wide eyes and hopped away into the undergrowth. Nate didn't imagine the way Cooper's entire body slumped.

Nate straightened up and wrapped a hand around Coop's wrist. "You okay?"

Cooper wouldn't meet his gaze. "I'm fine. Sometimes werewolves and wildlife don't mix, that's all. It was a...momentary aberration." Cooper pulled his hand out of Nate's grasp and walked back over to his bike. "Let's hit the beach." And with that he rode off down the road, leaving Nate to follow him while he wondered what the *fuck* that had been about.

All thoughts of werewolves and wildlife fled, though, when they reached their destination, because the bay was gorgeous. Once they'd parked their bikes and ditched their helmets, Nate stood at the top of the timber stairs that led to the beach and inhaled the sharp sea air as he took in the view.

The ocean was picture perfect, smooth and inviting and the sort of crystal-clear blue-green that was associated with tourist brochures advertising the Mediterranean or cruise ships. The odd pop of colour appeared on the surface, fluoro flippers breaking the surface with indelicate splashes as their owners dove down to the depths. Closer to shore, families played in the shallows. The sound of little kids squealing as they ran through the waves was synonymous with summer, as far as Nate was concerned.

A hand on his shoulder startled him out of his reverie. Cooper stood beside him, their backpacks hanging from one hand, and spent a few seconds gazing out over the water, his other hand resting at Nate's shoulder. Then he grinned and said, "Race you to the bottom."

He bolted down the stairs with Nate in hot pursuit, their thongs slap-slap-slapping against the wooden steps. When Nate reached the bottom, Cooper was waiting. He grabbed Nate by the waist and swung him through the air before depositing him on the sand, laughing. Whatever had been bothering him earlier, there was no sign of it now.

Cooper reached over and brushed Nate's hair away from his forehead where it was plastered with sweat from his bike helmet. Nate found himself leaning into the touch, chasing more. Cooper cupped his cheek, just for a second, and Nate soaked up the contact.

Cooper lifted his sunnies and settled them in his hair, frowning. "Your face is red. Are you sunburnt?"

Nate pressed a palm to his face, but there was none of the tell-tale sting that spoke of too long in the sun.

"Nah, I've got sunscreen on. I'm just red from biking in temperatures that belong in Satan's arsehole."

Cooper let out a snort at that, and they made their way down the beach. Once they'd stashed their gear in a shaded area, Nate peeled out of his singlet. He didn't miss the way Cooper's gaze roamed over him. He made sure to stretch his arms over his head so that his happy trail peeked out of his shorts before hanging his snorkel round his neck, kicking off his thongs and walking into the water with Cooper by his side.

As soon as it was deep enough, Nate dove forward, letting out a gasp as the cool water hit his overheated skin. It was just as exhilarating as he remembered, and he crawled in lazy strokes out into deeper waters, soaking up the warmth of the sun from above and the chill of the ocean below. Cooper kept pace, his arms slicing a wide arc through the water, before slipping his snorkel on and disappearing under the surface.

Nate pulled his own mask on. He always hated those first few seconds of snorkelling — he panicked at the lack of oxygen before he remembered to breathe through his mouthpiece — but it passed soon enough, as it always did, and he ducked his head under the water.

He spotted tiny flashes of neon as fish darted around underneath him. He grinned to himself as he followed them, their bright colours a blinking beacon as they caught the sunlight. Water lapped around his ears, a soothing backdrop as he gave a few languid kicks and let himself relax.

This really was paradise.

He lost track of time as he glided through the water, lifting his head above the surface now and again to make sure he hadn't drifted out too deep. Cooper floated right beside him, tapping his arm when he wanted to point at something interesting. The water was cool and clear, and Nate took in the sight of full-grown snapper swimming alongside other, more colourful species, flashes of silver darting in and out of the seagrass. Even when there wasn't anything that interesting to see, Nate still enjoyed losing himself in another world, the currents pulling him this way and that, rays of sunlight breaking through the surface and illuminating the sandy bottom in glittering patterns that were just as pretty as the myriad of colourful fish.

The high point of the day was when Nate spotted an octopus — or maybe a cuttlefish — hiding among the sea grass, and he reached out without thinking and grabbed Cooper's leg to alert him.

Cooper flailed and thrashed before he realised it was Nate. When he broke through the surface, he ripped his mask off, sputtering, "Fuck, I thought you were a shark!" His eyes were wide, and any trace of the cool, in-control businessman Nate had first met had vanished.

Nate pulled his own mask up, cackling at the sight of Cooper losing his shit. "Sharks don't have hands, Coop. Besides, I thought werewolves were tough, but you've been a real wuss today. Is it because you're a city wolf? Have you never seen nature before?"

Cooper drew in a couple of deep breaths, slicking wet hair out of his eyes in a way that gave Nate flashbacks to a porno involving a pool boy that he'd seen once. "You're a little shit, you know that?"

"So I've been told. There's an occy down there, by the way."

Cooper pulled his mask back into place and dipped back under the water. Nate joined him, watching in fascination as the creature rolled and slithered along the ocean floor before settling in a rock crevice.

When he surfaced again, Nate flipped over onto his back, closed his eyes, and let himself drift, content to let the current pull him along as he smiled to himself.

There was the sound of splashing. When Nate cracked an eyelid and turned his head, he saw that Cooper had also surfaced and rolled onto his back and was floating alongside him, his mask pulled down under his chin. He was watching Nate, the corners of his mouth curling up in a lazy smile, so Nate figured he was forgiven for calling Cooper a wuss.

Driven by an impulse he didn't quite understand, Nate reached out and clasped Cooper's hand, giving a light squeeze. Something in his chest settled when Cooper squeezed back. "Thanks for today, Coop. This was awesome."

"Anything for you, babe," Cooper said, the corners of his eyes creasing.

Nate gave his hand one more squeeze before letting go. The sun was right overhead, meaning he'd been in the water longer than he'd thought. He could feel the piercing heat of it on his skin even through the cool water. As much as he would have liked to have stayed floating next to Cooper and holding hands like a pair of otters — well, one otter and one wolf — experience had taught him that if he didn't want to be bright red later, he'd need another layer of sunscreen. "I'm heading in," he said, before flipping over and beginning a slow crawl back towards shore.

Cooper followed him in, and damn, he was a glorious sight striding out of the ocean. Rivulets of water ran down his chest and sunlight danced off the stray droplets on his skin, making him glisten. Nate forced himself to drag his gaze away, because the sand was too bloody hot to stand there gaping. With Cooper by his side, he enacted the time-honoured Australian ritual of dashing across the beach and swearing under his breath while hopping from foot to foot until he made it to where they'd stashed their gear in a shaded spot among large, smooth rocks.

They patted themselves dry, slipped their thongs on and donned their sunnies against the glare of the white sand. Nate dug the bottle of sunscreen from the bottom of his backpack. He was about to open the lid when Cooper reached out and took it from him. "Let me?"

Nate thought about those broad, smooth palms sliding up and down his back and his throat went tight. He swallowed, nodding, and sat down cross-legged on his beach towel in front of Cooper, leaning forward with his elbows on his knees.

The first drizzle of sunscreen between his shoulder blades was warm, and so was the hand that swept across his skin, spreading it slow and even up the back of Nate's neck and across his shoulders. Cooper applied another wide swathe right down his spine before his clever hands dipped low into the top of Nate's damp board shorts. Nate's skin tingled at the touch, and he let out a low moan as he sagged forward.

Cooper gave a pleased hum and continued rubbing the sunscreen in, his hands travelling over Nate's ribs in a smooth glide up then down again. It took all Nate's willpower not to turn and push Cooper onto his back, straddle his lap and kiss the hell out of him.

He managed to restrain himself, but only because there was a mum with two kids close by—a toddler puddling around in the shallows and a boy of around six in a lime green rashie who was knee deep in the water, jumping the tiny waves that were now lapping at shore. Nate wasn't going to be the dickhead who messed up a family day at the beach with a PDA.

Too soon, Cooper was handing him the tube of SPF 50, and Nate mourned the loss of his touch. Then Cooper ran a hand through his damp hair, tousled by sun and sea and salt, plopped himself down in front of Nate and said, "Do me?"

Nate would have done him with pleasure, but he knew that wasn't what Cooper meant. His brow creased. "I thought werewolves didn't get sunburn?"

Cooper tilted his head back, light reflecting off his sunnies, teeth gleaming as he grinned. "That doesn't mean wolves don't enjoy a pretty boy rubbing cream all over them, baby."

Well, that was an invitation if ever Nate had heard one. He squirted the sunscreen into his palm and dragged it across the seemingly endless breadth of Cooper's shoulders, leaving a white trail behind. He added more to both hands and swept up and down the length of his spine, drawing something out of Cooper that Nate was tempted to call a purr. Cooper's muscles were firm and enticing under his touch, and he let himself enjoy it, rubbing in the sunscreen and even dipping his fingers into the waist of Cooper's boardies and brushing at the soft skin there.

Cooper purred again, then he tensed, his gaze fixing on something.

"Coop?"

Nate followed his gaze. He barely had time to register that where there had been two little kids before, now there was one, before Cooper was rising to his feet in one fluid motion and sprinting down to the waterline and into the water, feet splashing as he ploughed through the surf with superhuman speed, gaze fixed on something — but what it was, Nate couldn't tell.

Just then, the mum leaped to her feet. "*Jayden?*"

Before Nate had time to connect the two occurrences, Cooper swerved to the left, bent down and scooped something up — a small, gasping, lime-green figure. He slung the kid over his shoulder and jogged back to shore looking like something out of *Baywatch* — if *Baywatch* were gay and starred werewolves.

*Baywolf.*

Cooper lifted Jayden off his shoulder and deposited him at his mother's feet, patting his back as the kid coughed and spat. Once Jayden was able to breathe, Cooper ruffled his hair, and Jesus, the sight of him with a small child *did* things to Nate.

"Little guy just lost his footing for a minute there," Cooper said. The mother crouched in front of her son, running her hands up and down him and squeezing him in a hug as Jayden snuffled and wailed and wiped saltwater snot across his face with the back of his hand. "He's fine."

"Thank you! Oh my God, I just looked away for a *second!* If you hadn't seen him…" Jayden's mum didn't loosen her grip on her son, but the adoring look she was giving Cooper had Nate's stomach twisting with possessiveness or maybe jealousy — or rather, what *would* have been jealousy, if Cooper had been his, instead of just a paid hook-up.

Cooper shrugged. "The sand drops off pretty quick there, and I heard him trying to call for help." He crouched and placed his palm against Jayden's chest, head cocked to one side. "His breathing and heart rate are good. I think he got more of a fright than anything. You're okay, right, mate?"

Jayden nodded, wide-eyed.

Cooper stood and ruffled Jayden's hair once more before striding back to Nate, leaving the mother to gather her kids close, squeezing and scolding Jayden in equal measure.

Nate stood and reached out his arms, because now *he* needed a hug. He shuddered as a long-buried memory came rushing back.

Cooper pulled him into an embrace. "Your heart's racing," he said. "You okay?"

The kid hadn't been in serious danger, not this time, but Nate knew from experience how that could all change in a split second. He closed his eyes against the flashback to his own childhood, of the time one half-decent wave had knocked him fair on his arse. The next thing he'd known he'd been dragged under, struggling to find his footing while trying to call for help, and inhaling water instead. Nate swallowed. "One too many close calls at Cottesloe as a kid, that's all."

Cooper tightened his arms around him, and the steady rhythm of his heartbeat under Nate's ear was soothing, steadying. Nate felt better almost at once. He heaved a sigh and pulled back, giving Cooper a wobbly smile. "I'm fine, I promise. And you were amazing. Like Aquaman, except hotter."

Cooper raised his eyebrows. "That's a very bold claim."

"I said what I said." Nate's smile was more genuine this time.

Cooper grinned and ran a hand through his damp hair, water flicking off the ends. "I'll take it." He glanced back at the ocean. "Did you want to go back in?"

Nate considered it. "Yeah, but not yet."

They sat on their spread beach towels, ate the protein bars from their backpack and drank their sports drinks. When they did go back in, they didn't bother with the snorkels, choosing to float in the shallows, splashing each other for fun, before deciding that it was time for a late lunch.

They dried themselves and donned their shirts. When Nate noticed Jayden's mum was also packing up, he offered to help, and she accepted with thanks. After they took a hand each, Nate helped her to swing-walk her toddler up the stairs while Cooper walked ahead with Jayden, carrying her stuff like it weighed nothing, muscles flexing under his singlet. Nate shoved down another burst of not-jealousy when he saw her checking out Cooper's arse.

It wasn't like he could blame her — not when he was doing the exact same thing.

They left her waiting for the island bus. He and Cooper cycled back to the settlement at Thompson Bay, taking their time. Nate snickered every time he saw a quokka at the side of the road. Cooper ignored him, eyes fixed forward.

They ate lunch at the pub. Since the weather was hot and the beer was crisp and cool, they stayed there for a while longer, drinking and talking and soaking up the relaxing vibes. Nate was enjoying himself far more than he'd hoped to when he'd first signed up for this. Cooper was quick to laugh at his jokes, throwing back his own one-liners. Was there anything sexier than a clever, funny man? Nate didn't think so.

Nate also noted how every eye in the place seemed to be drawn to Cooper. He couldn't help the pride that flooded him at the fact that the hottest man in the room had chosen *Nate* to spend his Companion time with.

If this were a normal day, he reflected as he drained his glass and gathered his backpack, he would have been mixing mortar and sweating his bollocks off. But instead, here he was living the dream, spending time with a hot guy, going to the beach and sitting at the pub. Later, they'd doubtless end up having more of the best sex of his life, and Cooper would say things about Nate being special and perfect and his, in a way that made Nate's stomach flutter and his nerves tingle in a way nobody had before.

It was just a shame it had to end.

# Chapter Six

Cooper watched Nate's mouth curl up into a tired smile as he gazed out of the window on the flight back. His wolf rumbled with satisfaction at the sight. His mate was relaxed and happy, which was as it should be.

Not that Nate *knew* he was Cooper's mate because Cooper hadn't told him yet, because he was a fucking coward. In his defence, it wasn't exactly the kind of news he could drop over a pint. Cooper *did* intend to tell him though…just as soon as he told him the other thing.

His lips thinned as he considered his options. Might it be better to tell Nate they were mates first? Then maybe it would be easier to explain why he'd somehow failed to mention that he was the CEO of the Shiftercorp Companion Programme. And depending how Nate took the news, he might even be able to gloss over the fact that he'd…not *cheated*, exactly, in his bid to win Nate for himself…but he *had* taken advantage of his position to make things go his way.

Maybe if he explained that he'd felt an undeniable pull when he saw Nate's profile, and that it was after the original bidder had fallen through that Cooper had felt compelled to make Nate his partner, Nate might even find it romantic.

And the thing was, it was true.

Once Cooper had seen Nate's picture, he'd been unable to shake the image of him. And when the first contract had fallen through, the chance to make Nate his, even for a week, had been irresistible.

He'd *needed* Nate as his companion, so he'd made it happen.

To her credit, Liz, his Perth Head of Operations, had been nothing but professional when he'd called her and told her he intended to acquire Nate for himself, and he didn't care what it took. While she'd agreed to organise a meeting, and even to play along with the fiction of Cooper being a random bidder, she'd also let Cooper know in no uncertain terms that she thought he should tell Nate the truth. She had reminded him that if Nate wasn't interested, then it didn't matter if Cooper was God himself, the partnership wouldn't go ahead.

He'd always liked Liz and admired her combination of warmth and practicality. In fact, he'd been so impressed at the backbone she'd shown in her insistence at sticking to the SCP guidelines that he'd arranged a salary increase to show his appreciation.

Luckily, Nate had been willing to give Cooper a chance, and now, after a single day and night together, Cooper couldn't imagine his life without Nate in it.

And now that his wolf had made him aware that Nate was his *mate*, the one person who could spark a fire in his belly and make his protective instincts come roaring to the fore—fuck, had Cooper threatened to kick a *quokka?* — he was faced with the question of how, and when, to tell Nate the truth.

The impatient, animal part of him wanted to shout it from the rooftops right now, claim Nate for his own before anyone else got a chance — but the sensible, strategic part of himself knew that he was better to wait, to spend this week convincing Nate that he wasn't just some blow-in who was here for a quick fuck. *Then* tell him that he wanted more.

As the helicopter descended, Nate flashed him a bright smile, and Cooper's heart clenched with possessiveness. He wondered if Nate felt the pull between them as well — some humans could, although it was rare.

Gods, he hoped so. It would make everything so much easier.

Once they landed, a car took them back to the hotel and satisfaction washed over Cooper when Nate reached out for his hand. Cooper let their palms rest together, and Nate gave him a crooked grin. His hair was a windswept mess, his cheeks were ruddy and his skin sparkled with traces of salt and sand.

Cooper wanted to devour him.

The car pulled in at the hotel and they got out. Nate's eyes were bright as he stretched, showing off a strip of belly skin in a way that *had* to be deliberate, and said, "I'm exhausted after all that swimming. I think I need a nap."

Cooper didn't need to hear the skip in Nate's heartbeat to know that it was a lie. The scent of lust was rolling off him in waves. "That so, baby?" he murmured, leaning in close as they made their way towards the bank of elevators, their boardies and sand-filled thongs incongruous among the marble grandeur. "Maybe I'll join you."

"Mmm, yes please," Nate said as he made a show of looking Cooper up and down. "That would be — "

"Mr Hudson?"

Cooper's head snapped around at Liz's voice. She was sitting on a small couch dwarfed by the vast foyer, a picture of elegance in a stylish summer dress with her ankles crossed, and she was holding a clipboard. She stood and walked over to them, expression apologetic. "I'm so, so sorry to interrupt your time together. I tried calling, but I got no reply."

Nate walked over, smoothing his singlet down over his exposed stomach. "Hey, Liz." His brow creased. "What's wrong?"

"Nothing's wrong, per se. It's just that I'm afraid that I missed one of the forms when you signed off yesterday. And the head of the SCP is positively *anal* about his paperwork."

Cooper choked on a mouthful of air and Liz sent him a wicked grin.

Nate shrugged. "Well, can we get it fixed up? Because I gotta say, I'm having the time of my life right now, and I don't want anything to get in the way. Right, Coop?" Nate settled his hand on Cooper's hip.

Cooper couldn't help himself. He leaned in towards Nate and pressed a kiss to his temple, the tang of ocean salt fresh against his lips. "Right, baby." He turned to Liz. "What do we need to sign?"

Liz turned the clipboard towards them and tapped a spot on the page, a standard NDA that had somehow been missed. "Right here…*Coop*."

Cooper signed and passed the clipboard over to Nate, not quite willing to meet Liz's eye.

Nate signed next, and Liz folded the top copy and handed it to him. Nate stuffed it into the pocket of his boardies. "Thank you, Nathan." She wrapped a hand around Cooper's elbow and said, "Now, would you mind if I steal a moment of Cooper's time? There are one or two admin details that I need to clarify with him, that's all."

Nate looked between them, something like jealousy flitting over his face. Cooper shouldn't have enjoyed seeing it there as much as he did. "Go on up, sweetheart. I'll just be a minute, and then I'll be all yours."

He gave Nate his most charming smile and raised one eyebrow in silent promise, pulling his elbow from Liz's grip, and was entertained to see Nate's features relax. So his boy *was* possessive. "Sure thing. I'll see you up there."

Nate grabbed his backpack and walked into the elevator. Once the doors had closed and there was no chance of Nate hearing them, Liz swung around to face him and prodded him in the chest with an elegant turquoise nail, her voice low so only he could hear. "Cooper Hudson, have you found your *mate*?"

Cooper's eyes widened and he wondered what had given him away. "What?"

"Your mate. It's obvious. I mean for starters, there's the way your expression goes all soft and gooey when you look at him. Not to mention the way you lean towards him like you're a dowsing rod and he's an underground stream."

"I—I—"

"You're doing it right now. You're staring at the lift doors like that will make him reappear. I remember the signs from when I met Brad."

Cooper considered denying it, before dismissing the idea. Liz wasn't stupid. He swallowed. "Yes. He's my mate."

Liz's smile stretched from ear to ear. "Oh, I'm so happy for you! There's no feeling like it in the world, is there? What did he say when you told him?"

"Um."

Liz gave him a stern glare. "You *have* told him, right?"

"I'm *going* to. But I only just figured it out myself last night. I'll tell him before the end of the contract, though, I swear. I just..." He sighed and ran a hand through his tousled hair. "How am I meant to drop that on him as *well* as the fact I'm the CEO of Shiftercorp? What if he doesn't believe me when I tell him we're mates?"

Liz fixed him with a look that said she thought he was an idiot. "If he's really your mate—"

"He *is*." Cooper growled. He'd never been more sure of anything in his life.

Liz gave a firm nod, as if she'd expected nothing less. "Then it's a once-in-a-lifetime bond. There will never be anyone else for you, as long as he's alive."

"I *know* that," Cooper interrupted. "Why do you think I'm so worried about fucking this up?"

Liz folded her arms across her chest, and Cooper knew what she was going to say before she opened her mouth. "Do you remember when you decided that you weren't going to tell Nate who you were when you chose him as your Companion, in case he thought you'd rorted the system? Which you did, but that's by the by."

Cooper's shoulders slumped and he made a non-committal sound.

"And do you remember how I said, 'You know, Cooper, maybe you *should* tell Nathan who you are and what you do, so this doesn't come back to bite you in the arse later'?"

"Uh huh," he said wearily. He'd hoped Liz had forgotten that particular conversation.

"How are those teeth feeling in that derriere right now, Mr Hudson?"

Cooper stared at his feet, noting the traces of sand still clinging to the tops of his toes, and sighed. "You were right," he admitted, "and I should have listened. But it doesn't answer the question of what I'm going to tell him, and how. I don't even know if he's aware that mates are a thing. What if he's one of those people who thinks it's a bullshit myth and accuses me of trying to enslave him?"

Liz's expression softened. "If he was one of those people, he would never have signed up for this. And if it helps, he does it too."

"Does what?"

"Looks at you like you hung the moon. Leans into you like a sunflower chasing the sun. Tracks your every move. Touches you without realising it. If I had to guess, I'd say he's feeling the bond as well. He just doesn't know it."

Cooper thought about the way Nate's hand had sought out his in the car, how he'd tangled their fingers in the water and the jealous expression on his face when Liz had touched Cooper's arm.

"You know what? It does help." He took a deep breath. "I like him, Liz, quite apart from the bond. He's funny, and he's smarter than he gives himself credit for and the things he does with his—"

"Aaand this is where I invent an excuse not to hear any more details of your sex life," Liz said, holding up a palm. "Go see your boy. And figure out how to convince him that you're it for him, like he is for you, before your contract expires and his profile opens up for other bids."

"*No.*" The low growl rumbled out of Cooper unbidden at the thought of anyone else getting their hands on his Nate. "Take him off the site."

Liz raised an eyebrow and placed a hand on his forearm. "Calm down, Cooper. I can't de-list his profile without his permission, but nobody's touching your boy. If you need more time to tell him, we can just extend your contract."

The fist of dread in Cooper's chest unclenched at that. *Yes.* He'd suggest that Nate sign on for more time while he courted him for real. And when the time was right, he'd explain about mates, and ask Nate to come home with him — for good.

\* \* \* \*

The elevator seemed to take forever, and Cooper found himself tapping his foot with barely suppressed impatience. He knew that the strength of his urge to be close to Nate was temporary and, like the flush of new love, would fade with time, but for now, it was almost overwhelming. He wanted to be near Nate — to touch him, hold him and claim him — and he had to remind himself that the smart move *wasn't* to burst through the door of their suite, declare his devotion and whisk Nate away like a fairy-tale princess. Not after one day.

No, he'd bide his time.

When he entered the suite, Nate was sprawled on the bed naked, sand still on his calves and bare feet, one arm thrown over his head. His eyes were closed and he looked utterly at peace. Cooper couldn't have stayed away if he'd wanted to. He stripped out of his own beach gear before sitting on the edge of the bed and leaning down to kiss Nate's cheek.

Nate scrunched his nose and squirmed before opening one eye. When he saw Cooper, his face split in a smile, and he propped himself up on his elbows. "Oh, hey! I was waiting for you so we could shower the sand off together."

"Mmmm. A shower does sound good." Cooper plopped down on the bed next to Nate and rolled so he was hovering over him on his elbows, caging him in, and leaned forward for a kiss as he savoured the heat of Nate's skin against his where they were pressed together.

Nate wrapped his arms around Cooper's neck and kissed him back. He tasted of the ocean and arousal, and Cooper's cock twitched at the heady combination. Nate pulled back and glanced down between their bodies, grinning, at the same time as his erection thickened against Cooper's thigh. "Maybe before we shower, you could get me dirty?" he said, rolling his hips.

"*Yes,*" Cooper growled low in his chest, and Nate's eyes went dark. Cooper pulled him in for another kiss before working his way down Nate's body, tugging and teasing at his nipple piercing, tracing over his tattoos with his tongue, mouthing at the soft skin of his belly, tasting every inch of ocean-salted skin that he could reach. When he reached Nate's now-straining cock, he licked the tip before raising his head. The floor-to-ceiling windows caught his eye, and he said, "I want to fuck you against the glass, baby."

"Absolutely not," Nate said, struggling up onto his elbows. "There's no way that glass is safety-rated for that, and I'm not ending up in *The Bell Tower Times* as 'Naked Man in shattering sexual experience at the Ritz.'"

"It's safe. It's double glazed," Cooper pointed out, his mind filled with images of Nate plastered against the glass as Cooper fucked him in front of the whole city, cementing his claim.

"It's not werewolf glazed, though," Nate said, the corner of his mouth twitching, and Cooper just *knew* he was thinking back to their first time together.

"Oh, you want a glazed werewolf?" Cooper said, raising an eyebrow and grinning. Then he took Nate's cock all the way into his mouth.

Nate gave a shout, his back arching, and Cooper's mouth flooded with the tang of pre-cum. He sucked at Nate's cock, head bobbing and throat working as he took Nate deep. He didn't slow down until Nate was shaking, tiny tremors running through his entire frame—and when Nate *did* come, Cooper didn't swallow. Instead he pulled off and, closing his eyes, let the warm stripes of cum hit his face and neck as he wrapped a hand around Nate's shaft and milked him dry.

Nate collapsed back against the bed, breathing hard. When he looked at Cooper through heavy-lidded eyes, his pupils were blown wide. "Fuck, why is seeing you marked up like that so hot?"

"Maybe you like claiming me as yours," Cooper said, before licking the cum off his bottom lip.

Nate's breathing hitched. "Fuck, yeah. That's probably it."

He reached over and ran a thumb down Cooper's cheekbone, through the mess there. "Jesus, seeing you like this makes me want you inside me. Like, right now."

"My pleasure, baby," Cooper purred, while his wolf danced with joy at the thought that Nate wanted to claim him.

He didn't waste time, opening Nate up with slick fingers and sliding inside in one smooth stroke. It was like coming home. The velvet softness of Nate's insides as Cooper rutted into him, combined with the little *unh-unh-unh* sounds he made with every thrust, drove Cooper wild with the need to claim him. He gave into the urge to lean in and suck at the soft skin on the curve of Nate's neck, nipping at the spot where his claiming bite would go.

Nate let out a broken moan, his arse clenching reflexively, and it had Cooper's balls drawing up tight. He gripped Nate around the waist and fucked into him once more, *hard*, and seconds later his release hit him like a freight train. His hips stuttered and that familiar lightning raced down his spine, pleasure washing over him and his cock pulsing as Nate moaned and gasped under him in a way that was nothing short of intoxicating.

After he'd ridden out the aftershocks, Cooper buried his face in the crook of Nate's neck and rolled them to their sides. Nate squirmed when Cooper's softening cock slipped out of him while Cooper soaked up their combined scents. He would have been happy to stay there in a tangle of limbs, except the cum on his face was starting to feel decidedly unpleasant as it dried.

He sat up, and when he looked down and took in the fucked-out expression on Nate's face, satisfaction coursed through him that he'd been the one to put it there.

Nate grinned up at him. "See something you like?"

"You look wrecked, and it suits you."

"Well, you can wreck me anytime you'd like — at least, you can for the rest of the week."

Cooper's gut clenched, and he had to remind himself that Nate didn't mean anything by it, that he didn't *know* that he was Cooper's mate, because Cooper hadn't told him about the existence of mates yet. But he would.

He just had to hope he didn't fuck it up.

# Chapter Seven

"So, this isn't a complaint, but are we staying the entire week at the Ritz, or did you have something else planned?" Nate grimaced. "Wow. That sounds super Veruca Salt. *Are we* only *going to the Ritz, Daddy?*"

Someone at the next table swung around and stared. Cooper's eyebrow rose into his hairline, which was when Nate realised just how that had sounded. He groaned and propped his elbows on the table of the hotel restaurant, burying his face in his hands.

Deft fingers peeled his hands away from his face, and Cooper grinned at him. "It's fine, Nate. I got the reference. And in answer to your question, I'm hoping to spend a couple of nights in the Swan Valley. Liz is getting us a booking for tomorrow night at a werewolf-owned winery." He paused, the corner of his mouth quirking up. "The chalets have soundproofing."

Nate hid his face again. "Oh *God*. Is that because of this morning?"

"Baby, I love the noises you make, but you were *loud*," Cooper teased, his smile widening enough that the corners of his eyes creased attractively. "I took it as a compliment."

Nate thought back to their early morning antics. They'd been fooling around in the shower, and Cooper had lifted him clear off the floor and fucked him against the wall, long and hard. Nate's shouts had echoed off the tiles, loud enough that he was certain the entire floor must have heard him when he'd come his brains out—twice.

Nate assumed that was the reason for the judgemental stares they'd gotten from the couple in the next room when they'd shared the elevator down to the lobby.

Worth it, in his opinion.

He went back to eating his poached eggs and wondered again what kind of influence Cooper had, that not only was he important enough to get accommodation at the peak of summer—Rottnest notwithstanding—but that the head of Shiftercorp's WA operations was bending over backwards to keep him happy. But he bit back the urge to ask if Cooper was a mafia kingpin, even as a joke, because he got the sense that whatever it was, Cooper wasn't keen to talk about it—and in all honesty, he wasn't sure if he wanted to know.

It wasn't like it mattered. He wasn't going to see Coop again, anyway.

His stomach soured and he pushed his plate away.

Cooper's brow furrowed. "Nate? What's wrong? You look pale."

"Nothing." Nate bit his lip to keep from blurting out that he wanted this to last longer, because in all likelihood all that would just send Cooper running for the hills. He forced a smile. "That last bite of egg's sitting wrong, that's all."

Cooper looked unconvinced, and Nate remembered too late that his heartbeat would have given away his lie in, well...a heartbeat. Cooper didn't call him on it, though. Instead, he reached across the table and took Nate's hand, giving it a squeeze. An unaccountable warmth bloomed in Nate's chest, replacing his unease. Cooper pushed his own plate aside and drained his coffee cup, checking his watch. "Shall we walk up to Hay Street?"

"Yeah, that sounds good," Nate said. "I don't come into the city much."

Cooper's hand sought his as they meandered through the streets, their casual pace a contrast to the smart-suited flood of young professionals with their Bluetooth earpieces and set expressions who were marching towards their destinations.

Nate was reminded *why* he didn't come into the city much after the third person elbowed him as they pushed past. He let out a grunt and muttered, "Bloody hell."

Cooper had his arm around Nate's waist in an instant, pulling him close and steering him down a laneway that was much less crowded. "Better?" he asked, not letting go as he gazed into Nate's face before brushing a stray piece of hair behind his ear.

It was kind of sweet, and also kind of ridiculous. "It's fine, Coop."

Cooper pursed his lips. "I don't like people touching what's—" He snapped his mouth shut and cleared his throat, pointing down the laneway. "This looks interesting. Mind if we poke around down here?"

It was such a sad attempt to hide his protectiveness that Nate didn't have the heart to call him on it. Instead he nodded, and let Cooper lead the way.

They passed coffee shops, a bookshop, a nail salon and a place that sold Bali fashions before stopping outside a tiny art gallery that was also a jeweller's and deciding to go in. Nate got lost in the artist's work for a while, the art on display there a combination of modern and quirky, before wandering through to the jewellery display room.

There was one ring in particular that caught his eye, captivating him. It was a sleek platinum band, engraved with stylised lines denoting werewolves all the way around. He had a sudden urge to buy it for Cooper—which was *ridiculous*. As nice as the ring was, Cooper didn't want or need a present from Nate.

Yet somehow, after ensuring Cooper was nowhere in sight, Nate found himself buying it anyway, and not even blinking at the price tag.

It was *made* for Coop, and Nate was meant to give it to him—that was all there was to it.

The owner of the gallery gave a pleased smile as she put the ring in its box then put it into an organza bag. Nate guessed he'd be smiling too, if someone had just dropped the amount he had.

He slipped the bag into the pocket of his cargo shorts and looked around for Cooper, but by the time he'd circled the gallery and come back to the front desk, he was still nowhere in sight. "Your friend went outside. He was looking for you," the owner said, still beaming.

"Thanks." Nate stepped out through the door and found Cooper a few feet up the laneway, sitting on a bench. He waved, and Cooper's eyes lit up. He rose to his feet with the innate grace that all werewolves possessed and held out his hand. Nate took it, unquestioning. It was like the ring—it felt *right*.

"Did you get lost in there?" Cooper teased.

"Uh huh. The owner was trying to persuade me to be the muse for her next sculpture, so I had to hide in a cupboard."

Cooper hummed. "You'd look good in marble. Sleek."

"Damn straight," Nate said, grinning.

"Sweetheart, we both know that there's not a single thing about you that's straight," Cooper shot back. Nate threw back his head and laughed.

They wandered around the city for a while longer window shopping, Nate stopping to pick up a Lotto ticket, before the heat of the day started to set in. Sweat beaded at Nate's temples and his shirt was sticking to his back. "It's too bloody hot for this," he said. "Let's sit down somewhere."

"I was thinking the same thing." Cooper steered Nate into the closest café. Nate didn't miss the way his hand settled in the small of Nate's back.

He didn't hate it.

They found a table and Cooper went and ordered them each a mango smoothie. While he was gone, Nate put his hand in his pocket to check that the ring was still there. He'd been going to give it to Cooper tonight, but he decided he'd give it to him now instead. He couldn't wait to see Cooper's face when he opened it.

And if he happened to fantasise how the metal would look gleaming against the tan skin of Cooper's hand while he jacked Nate off, well, that was his business.

Cooper slipped into the seat opposite him. There was a tense set to his shoulders that hadn't been there before. "Everything okay?"

Cooper swallowed and tugged at the throat of his V-neck, revealing tan skin and a trace of chest hair. "I, ah."

Nate frowned. "What's wrong?"

Cooper ran a hand through his hair. "Nothing. Nothing's *wrong*. I, um." He made a frustrated sound before reaching into his pocket and pulling out a flat black rectangular box. "I hope you don't mind but I got you something," he said, sliding it across the table.

Nate reached out and took the box. The logo on the lid matched the one on the box in his pocket, and he ran his fingers over the edges, mouth curving into a smile. "For me?"

Cooper leaned forward in his seat, hands clasped in front of him. "I just... I saw it, and I needed you to have it. Is that okay?"

Nate thought of his own compulsion to buy the ring for Cooper and nodded in understanding. He eased the top edge of the box up, and the hinge snapped open. Nate let out a soft, *"Oh,"* when he saw what was nestled against the satin lining.

It was an elegant hand-crafted silver wolf's head pendant, hanging from a braided leather cord with a small silver clasp. It was gorgeous. He lifted it from the box and held it in the palm of his hand, taking in the incredible level of detail, from the topaz stones for eyes to the individually etched hairs on the tips of the ears.

He loved it an unreasonable amount.

He held the hand with the pendant out to Cooper. "Put it on me?"

Cooper nodded, giving a pleased smile. He came and stood behind Nate's chair and fastened the clasp. Nate would have been lying if he said he didn't feel a little bit like Julia Roberts right then—except Cooper left Richard Gere in the dust, in his opinion. The pendant sat solid and reassuring against his throat, like a claim and a promise.

Cooper trailed his fingertips down Nate's throat, breathing out a whispered, "Gorgeous."

"Yeah." Nate's voice caught. "It is."

"I meant you, baby," Cooper said, and in that moment, Nate believed him utterly.

He put his hand over Cooper's and gave a light squeeze. "Is this why you disappeared in that shop?"

"Yeah, I snuck out the back. I wanted it to be a surprise." Cooper removed his hand from Nate's and sat back down as the waiter arrived with their drinks. "So you like it, then?"

"I fucking love it." He stuck his hand in his pocket and pulled his own gift bag out and placed it on the table between them. "But also it explains why the artist seemed so entertained when I got this. She must think we're a pair of saps, buying each other gifts."

Cooper froze, eyes wide. "You...got me a gift?" He sounded shocked.

"I saw it, and I needed you to have it," Nate echoed. "Just because." Cooper remained silent and Nate bit his lip, worried that he'd somehow insulted Cooper or broken some secret werewolf rule. "Is that okay? Because if it's not I can take it back—"

"No! No, it's fine," Cooper said hastily, pulling the bag towards himself. "It's wonderful."

"You don't know that," Nate said, growing nervous. "You might hate it."

Cooper lifted his gaze from the bag, and Nate saw that his face was wreathed in smiles. "Nate, do you know how long it's been since anyone got me a gift *just because*?"

Judging from the way he was still beaming, Nate guessed it had been a while. But of course, if Cooper *was* some sort of mob boss, it made sense. Any gift he received doubtless came from obligation or a need to win his favour.

Except, the more time they spent together, the harder Nate was finding it to imagine Cooper as a kingpin. He wasn't ruthless or uncaring. Hell, he'd rescued a little kid from drowning yesterday. And his phone had remained silent after that one call yesterday, so maybe he was just an investment banker, or the national head of a Tupperware division or some shit like that.

Cooper was fidgeting with the drawstrings on his gift bag, almost like he was waiting for permission, so Nate said, "Go on, open it. And if it's shit, lie and tell me you like it anyway."

Cooper opened the bag and drew out the ring box, stroking the lid reverently before he opened it. He drew in a sharp breath, looking from the box to Nate and back to the box again, before sliding the ring from its confines and running a thumb over the etchings. "This is—" Cooper's throat worked as he swallowed, and he ran the heel of the hand not holding the ring over his eyes. "Shit, Nate."

He looked overwhelmed, and Nate didn't know what to do with that, so he deflected. "Was that, *'This is shit, Nate?'* or *'Shit, this is awesome, Nate?'* You'll have to clarify so I know whether I fucked up or not."

"Not," Cooper said, his voice thick. "You did *not* fuck up." He slid the ring onto the third finger of his right hand, and it was a perfect fit, like it had been made for him. He gave Nate a tremulous smile and said, "So, does it make me shallow if I say that this very pretty gift makes me want to take you back to the hotel and ruin you?"

"Well, if it does, then that makes two of us," Nate said, because the sight of Cooper wearing his gift was doing strange things to him, stirring a hunger deep in his belly. He had a sudden deep yearning to lay himself bare, expose his throat and let Cooper take charge.

He tilted his head to one side, trailed a finger down the leather string of his new pendant and said in a low voice, "You can do whatever you want with me, Coop."

Cooper's smile widened, became more confident, and he drained his glass in one swallow. "Drink up, baby. I need you hydrated for what I have planned."

Nate grinned back, finished his smoothie and said, "Lead the way."

\* \* \* \*

"Baby?" A warm hand shook Nate's shoulder. He rolled over and blinked awake to find Cooper sitting on the side of the bed looking down at him, a fond smile on his face. Nate didn't even remember falling asleep, but that wasn't surprising. Cooper leaned down and kissed his cheek, running one hand through Nate's bedhead, and warmth bloomed in Nate's chest at the show of affection. "I ordered room service for dinner. I didn't think you'd be up for going out."

He was wearing a pair of cargo shorts and nothing else. Nate couldn't help running a palm over the muscled planes of his stomach, his hand coming to rest on Cooper's hip. "How long was I asleep?"

Cooper shrugged. "A couple of hours." He grinned, looking far too pleased with himself. "I think I broke you, baby."

"I think you did too. Worth it." Nate stretched and yawned, wincing at the deep throb in his arse—a reminder of just what they'd done when they'd gotten back to the hotel.

Led by some unfathomable instinct, he'd knelt naked—except for his new pendant—at Cooper's feet, and silently bared his throat. And Cooper?

Cooper had let the wolf out.

Nate could still feel the echo of Cooper's cock in his arse where he'd fucked Nate like a man possessed, and Nate's thighs burned from where he'd ridden Cooper like a mechanical bull the second time around.

The sex had been primal and unrestrained, a wild and desperate thing, and Nate had enjoyed every minute of it—but he also couldn't see himself moving anytime soon, let alone making himself respectable for dinner.

He rolled onto his back and noted that someone had cleaned him up—Cooper, obviously—and a wave of affection washed over him for the man who was thoughtful enough to wipe the jizz off him while he slept, and considerate enough to arrange room service.

God, he wished this didn't have to end.

His gut twisted at the realisation that he only had three more days of this before Cooper would be gone forever. It was like a bucket of cold water being thrown over him, extinguishing his good mood. He forced himself upright, chest tightening as sick anticipation filled him, his breaths shallow and forced.

"Nate?" Cooper put a hand on his shoulder, and Nate wanted to shrug it off, but he couldn't quite bring himself to—and that was the problem right there, wasn't it? Cooper was like a drug, and Nate was addicted. Even now, the heat of his hand on Nate's skin calmed him down, easing the pressure in his chest and making it a little easier to breathe. "Baby, what's wrong? Are you okay?"

Nate breathed in and out, slow and steady, before answering. He *intended* to say he was fine, but instead what came out of his mouth was, "I don't want this week to end."

*What the fuck, brain?*

He waited for Cooper to raise those sexy eyebrows in judgement and make some comment about 'all good things must come to an end' or wherever the hell else shifters said to placate their too-clingy companions, but instead Cooper smiled, slow and easy. Nate could have sworn he looked *pleased* at Nate's confession.

His impression was confirmed when Cooper said, "I'm glad, baby. Because I was going to ask if you wanted to extend your contract?" He cupped Nate's face in one palm. "I'd appreciate it if I could keep you, at least a little longer."

Nate's heart pounded and his mind whirled. He was torn between celebrating and running for the hills. He wanted to say yes, to stay and delay their parting, but like any addiction, he could just imagine that the longer he put off quitting, the worse his withdrawals would be. The thought of being apart from Cooper already made him feel physically sick.

Cooper's eyes were wide and hopeful, and his hand was warm and reassuring. Nate couldn't help but shake the feeling that he was right where he was meant to be—which must have been his body pulling some sort of post-coital emotional bullshit.

This was a short-term gig by design.

Staying longer, however tempting, was just putting off the inevitable. He took a deep breath. "I don't think I can."

Cooper furrowed his brow. "Nate?" He withdrew his hand and clasped both in his lap, looking down. "There's no obligation if you don't want to extend. I just..." Cooper fell silent.

"Just what?"

Cooper stood, walking over to the windows. "Nothing. It's fine. We see out the week, no hard feelings."

Even with his back turned to Nate, the slump in his shoulders was obvious, and Nate hated seeing it with every fibre of his being.

He slid out of bed and went to stand next to Cooper, drawn like iron filings to a magnet, overcome with an inexplicable need to comfort his wolf.

*His* wolf?

No. Cooper wasn't *his* anything, no matter how much Nate wanted it — and he *did* want it. And wasn't that a punch to the gut?

He tried to imagine spending the next three days pretending he was fine, pushing down this growing, incessant need to beg Cooper to stay, while waiting to say goodbye — and he couldn't.

If he wanted any chance of getting over Cooper, he needed to walk away now.

That didn't stop him slipping his arms around Cooper's waist and plastering himself against his back, allowing himself to feel the comfort and security that seemed to emanate from him and seep into Nate's very core.

Cooper let out a soft sigh and *God*, Nate wanted to stay right here, to take Cooper up on his offer of extra time, and soak up enough of him to last a lifetime.

But he didn't. Instead, telling himself it was better this way, he pulled away and, eyes stinging, forced the words out. "I need to leave."

Cooper froze before turning on his heel. *"What?"*

Nate blinked back tears and, his voice shaking, said, "I said, I need to leave." He stepped back from Cooper, ignoring the way all of his senses were screaming that this was a mistake. "Am I calling an Uber, or can Liz collect me?"

Cooper's mouth dropped open, and Nate's chest tightened at the devastation that was written across his face. Cooper swallowed, throat working, before he whispered, "What did I do?"

And what the hell was Nate supposed to say to that?

# Chapter Eight

Time stood still.

Cooper stared at Nate, heart pounding, as he tried to make sense of what he was hearing. In the space of a heartbeat, they'd gone from Nate not wanting the week to end to Nate demanding to leave. Cooper didn't have the faintest idea what had happened to change his mind.

When Cooper had taken a chance and bought the pendant for Nate, he'd known that the exchange of jewellery or trinkets was the first tentative step in a werewolf courtship, but *Nate* hadn't—yet he'd returned the gesture anyway, with the ring he'd purchased.

Then, when he'd made that comment about not wanting the week to end, Cooper had been convinced that Nate was feeling the bond. So he'd offered to extend the contract, thinking Nate would leap at the chance. But now Nate was—Nate was *leaving*, and Cooper didn't understand *why* he was leaving.

He was *Cooper's.*

His wolf prowled, restless and angry just beneath the surface, ready to pounce, to pin Nate down and make him stay, to insist that they belonged together and claim him there and then. Cooper was keeping it reined in—just—but his control was hanging by a thread. He closed his eyes and breathed deep, balling his hands into fists at his sides and ignoring the sting of emerging claws as he asked again, "What did I *do*, Nate?"

Nate half-stepped, half-stumbled backward, his emotions rolling off him in a wild, roiling cloud, and Cooper almost choked on the stench of his sorrow.

Wait.

His *sorrow*?

Why was Nate upset when he was the one asking to leave? It didn't make sense—but it was enough to stop Cooper's burgeoning panic in its tracks. If Nate didn't really want to leave, maybe Cooper could still turn this around—and God, he hoped he could, because looking at Nate with his face pale, his eyes shining with tears, naked and vulnerable and coming apart at the seams, Cooper wanted nothing more than to protect him, to cherish him and yes, to love him.

He took a breath and retracted his claws before taking a careful step forward, extending a hand, palm up. "Baby? Talk to me."

Nate turned his back and started pulling on his clothes in quick, jerky movements. "The contract says I can walk away. I'm walking away." Despite the bravado in his voice, despair tinged his scent.

"I'm not trying to stop you, baby," Cooper said, ignoring the voice in his head that called him a dirty liar. "I just want to understand. Was it something I said, something I did?"

"You—" Nate's voice was low as he grabbed his duffel and tossed it on the bed, yanking his clothing from the drawers and stuffing it in. "You can't just say shit like that, not when you don't mean it."

"Shit like what?"

Nate turned to face him, chest heaving. "*Romantic* shit. Calling me 'baby'. Saying that you want to *keep* me. It's not fair, not when I—" His mouth snapped shut, and Cooper could hear his heart thundering in the sudden silence.

An idea started to form, a possible reason for Nate's about-face, but he pushed it aside, unwilling to take a chance on hope just yet. "Nate," he tried again. "I just want to make you happy."

All the fight left Nate at once. He sat down next to his bag and buried his face in his hands. He reeked of misery and confusion, and Cooper wanted nothing more than to scoop Nate up in his arms and comfort him, heedless of the ache in his own chest.

He settled for crouching in front of him and brushing the hair out of his eyes before resting his palm against Nate's heart, eyes closed as he memorised the steady thump-thump-thump against his palm through the thin fabric of Nate's shirt—because if Nate *was* leaving, Cooper needed to touch him this one last time.

After all, the memory would have to last him a lifetime.

Nate raised his head and sighed. "Why do you have to be so fucking *nice?*" He clasped his hand over Cooper's, and it rested there, the touch a balm to Cooper's soul—until Nate stiffened and pulled his hand away like he'd been burnt. "See? I can't help— you're too—"

"Too *what*, Nate?" If Nate wanted to leave, Cooper sure as hell wouldn't keep him against his will. But he needed some answers, for the sake of his own sanity, and he wasn't sure he could wait for Nate to figure out how to tell him. He sat on the bed next to him. "Let me hold you, baby, and then you can tell me what the *hell* is going on."

He lifted Nate with no effort, hauling him into place so that he was straddling Cooper's lap, and Nate didn't object. Instead he buried his head against Cooper's shoulder with a sigh, which Cooper took as a good sign.

He let a hint of the wolf creep into his tone when he said, "Now, talk."

Nate's breath was warm against the curve of his throat as he inhaled, nuzzling Cooper's throat. Cooper let out a soft moan, and Nate stiffened before pulling back, his whole body a tense line. "*Fuck.*"

He scrambled out of Cooper's lap, stumbling backward, chest heaving, and pointed at Cooper with a trembling finger. "*This.* This is why I can't stay."

Cooper tilted his head to one side, considering what he wanted to say next. He had his suspicions, and fuck, he hoped he was right, but sometimes it was all about asking the right questions. "Nate," he said, voice soft, "tell me why you want to leave."

Nate stared at him wide-eyed. His breathing hitched, and it looked like he was struggling with himself before he mumbled. "The contract says I can go. It doesn't matter why."

Cooper caught his gaze. "It matters to me. *You* matter to me."

"Yeah, right," Nate muttered. "For this week."

Oh. *Oh.*

"This doesn't make any sense, Nate." But it was beginning to, if Cooper was choosing to be optimistic — and he'd always been optimistic. His earlier suspicion returned, stronger this time, and with it came a burst of hope that refused to be denied. "Do you *want* to leave?"

Nate bit his lip. "I think I need to."

His heartbeat skipped.

Cooper forced himself to remain calm. "Need and want aren't the same thing, baby. Why do you *need* to leave?"

Nate plopped down on the small leather sofa opposite Cooper and set his elbows on his knees, twisting his hands together.

Cooper moved from his sofa, so he was next to Nate. He brushed his lips along Nate's temple, a lover's caress, and, heart thundering, asked the important question. "Is this because you're feeling things you think you shouldn't feel?" he murmured low in his ear. "Getting too attached?"

Nate stiffened, and Cooper waited, until —

"Yes!" Nate burst out. "Fucking *yes*, okay? I can't stop thinking about you, and it's like you're under my fucking *skin*, and it's stupid, because we've known each other *two days*, but I like you too much. Fuck, I think I might even love you, and I don't know what I'll do once this is over!" He turned to Cooper, eyes welling with tears, and his voice was hoarse. "I—I don't think I *can* stay any longer. I have to go while I can, because otherwise — otherwise, it just might break me when you leave."

His eyes widened, and he slapped his hands over his mouth like he wanted to take the words back, expression horrified.

"Oh, baby," Cooper said, voice hoarse, his heart clenching in sympathy for the confusion Nate had suffered, all because he'd been too chickenshit to tell him the truth. "I *love* you. I'm never leaving you."

Nate stared at him for a second, then comprehension dawned and he breathed out, "Oh, thank *fuck*," and surged forward. Cooper met him in the middle, unable to hold himself back. Somehow Nate was sprawled across the couch on his back and Cooper was kissing the fuck out of his mate. Nate kissed him back, hands tangling in Cooper's hair, his scent transforming from bitter to honey-sweet as the kiss went on. When Cooper pulled back, Nate's smile threatened to split his face in half. "Is this real?" he asked, breathless, caressing the nape of Cooper's neck.

"It's real," Cooper assured him, even though he wasn't quite convinced himself. His heart raced — part relief, part adrenaline and part lust. "You're mine, baby."

Nate's eyes were alight with wonder. "Is it... Am I your... Are we mates?"

Cooper sat up, because this wasn't a conversation he should have with Nate pinned under him, as tempting as it was to keep him there. "You know about mates?"

Nate sat up and straddled Cooper's lap, pressing their foreheads together. "A little bit. I know they're real." He let out a soft sigh. "I've been so fucking confused, Coop. I wanted you like air, and I didn't know why."

Cooper cupped Nate's jaw and tilted his head so he could look him in the eye. "I'm so, so sorry, baby. I planned to tell you, I swear, but it happened so fast, and I didn't want to just drop it on you. If I'd known you were feeling the bond too, I would have said something."

He smoothed a palm down Nate's spine, and Nate relaxed under his touch. "So, how long have you known?" Nate asked.

"I realised yesterday. The pendant was the start of my courting you."

Nate grinned. "Courting me, huh? Is that just a fancy term for being my boyfriend?"

Cooper huffed out a laugh. Nate was taking this far better than he'd hoped. "I guess it is. Although with mates, it's more intense — as you've already discovered."

"Oh yeah, you're it for me, Coop, no question. It's like the ring. There was no doubt that it was meant to be yours. Just like I am."

Cooper caught his breath. "Is that a yes to being my mate?"

"Was it even a question?" Nate said with a raised eyebrow. "Mates are mates are mates, it feels like. I don't think I *could* say no. And I don't want to, because damn, Coop. You're sexy as fuck, smart as hell and I like you. I mean, I think I love you, but I *like* you as well, which is a separate thing. So yes, I'll be your mate."

Cooper's chest bloomed with warmth. While he was still revelling in the sensation, Nate kissed him and rolled his hips, the combination of his plush mouth and firm body making Cooper's cock twitch.

It took all his willpower to pull back, but Cooper knew that he needed to tell Nate everything, be sure he knew what he was signing up for before they went any further. He took a deep breath. "Nate, there's something else. It's my job."

Nate stilled, and a frisson of nervousness entered his scent. "Is it...illegal?"

Cooper furrowed his brow. "No?"

Nate relaxed. "Then does it matter? Like, if you're not an underworld boss or a drug runner or a hired killer, I'm good." He placed a series of delicate kisses down the curve of Cooper's jaw, teeth scraping the skin in a way that made Cooper want to throw him down on his back and fuck him right there, talking be damned. But he'd come too close to losing Nate to risk any more misunderstandings.

He guided Nate's head away from his throat with a gentle hand, ignoring the way his wolf whined at the delay in claiming him, and said, "It's important. I'm the CEO of Shiftercorp."

"The CEO of Shiftercorp. Huh." Nate gazed at Cooper, eyes dark, and traced his tongue over his bottom lip. "Yay for you, I guess?" Then he went back to kissing down Cooper's jawline.

Cooper swallowed when Nate mouthed down his throat, and it took everything in him to pull him away again with a hand on the back of his neck. "No, Nate. You need to know something. I saw you, and I needed you. So I made it happen."

"And?"

"It wasn't right, and I don't want any more secrets between us."

Nate sat up straight and sighed. "Whatever this is has you tied up in knots, doesn't it?"

Cooper nodded, his heart racing.

Nate arched an eyebrow. "Two questions. Did you actively fuck over someone else's bid to hire me?"

"No! Your original bidder couldn't pay. But I *did* dress it up as a glitch to get my bid in."

Nate nodded. "Okay, I can deal with that. Second question. Have you done it before?"

"I've never taken a companion before you."

Nate tilted his head to one side. "Huh. So you're telling me that the one time you've taken advantage of your position, it was because of me?" His face broke into a wide smile. "That's as flattering as fuck, Coop. Now if you don't mind, can I get back to kissing my sexy *mate*?"

He rolled the word 'mate' around on his tongue, and hearing it come out of his mouth had Cooper fighting the urge to claim him right there, but there was one last thing he needed to clarify. "Nate, I have to ask — would you consider taking my mating bite? It won't turn you, but it secures us to each other."

Nate arched one eyebrow. "Cooper Hudson, I don't think you're getting the memo. Whatever being your mate involves, I'm in. I want it all. I want *you*."

Fuck, Cooper loved this glorious boy.

He gave in to his impulse to bury his face in the curve of Nate's throat, licking at the skin. "Here. I'd bite you right here."

Nate shuddered and let out a filthy moan. "Is it normal that I want to take you to bed and fuck you stupid right now?"

"Absolutely. The bond is intense." Cooper purred against Nate's neck, his dick throbbing.

Nate tilted his head up and away, sitting back. "No, Coop. Listen. I want to fuck *you*." He hesitated. "Is that something you do?"

Although it wasn't something Cooper did *often*, his cock throbbed and a low rumble came from deep in his chest, his wolf rejoicing at the thought of Nate being the one to fill him, claiming him inside and out. He rasped out, "It is when it's you, baby."

"Your fucking *voice*," Nate breathed. "Can't wait to hear you begging when I fuck you." He pulled Cooper in for a frantic, messy kiss, and the taste of him was intoxicating, his scent swirling with notes of arousal and excitement.

Cooper couldn't bear to wait any longer. He stood in one fluid motion, with Nate wrapping his legs around him like a koala, and carried him through to the bedroom, dropping Nate on the bed with a soft whoosh as the feather doona billowed out under him. He turned away long enough to kick his cargos and boxer briefs off, and when he turned back, Nate had stripped bare as well and was propped up against the headboard, one hand wrapped around his sizeable erection.

Cooper couldn't wait to feel the length of it inside him. He got onto the bed next to Nate, rolled onto his back, threw his arms out to the side and said, "Be gentle with me."

It was meant as a tease, but Nate propped himself up on one elbow, his expression tender, and said, "Always, Coop."

When Nate rolled over and kissed him, it was soft and sweet and lazy. Nate's hand against his skin was gentle as he ran it down Cooper's side and along his flank in a sweeping motion. Cooper melted into the sensation and let Nate take charge.

Nate's scent bloomed rich with arousal and anticipation, but his touches were careful, reverent. He kissed down Cooper's throat and across his pecs, teasing Cooper's nipples until they were tight and tingling and Cooper couldn't hold back his moans, before sliding his hand down Cooper's abs at last, and touching his cock. His grip was sure, his palm broad and hot, the ghost of calluses past a delicate rasp against sensitive skin, and Cooper found himself rocking up into the touch, panting with need. "Fuck, Nate."

"We'll get there, baby," Nate murmured. Hearing the pet name out of Nate's mouth sent a burst of want racing through Cooper's veins. He fucked up into Nate's grip, and when Nate took his hand away, he whined. Nate gave a soft laugh. "Need my hand to get you ready, babe."

With that, he pressed Cooper's knees up and apart and ran a slick finger over his hole. When had he even grabbed the lube? Cooper didn't know, and it didn't matter. All his attention was focused on the slip-slide of a fingertip against his arse, nudging and teasing at the nerve endings. Nate slipped one finger inside him and set up a steady rhythm, tugging at his rim to open him further. It was overwhelming, addictive, and Cooper closed his eyes and lost himself to it, tugging at his cock and soaking up the dual sensations of his own hand and Nate's working him over. One finger became two as Nate opened him up, the fleeting sting soon forgotten when Nate hooked his fingers and grazed Cooper's prostate, making him shout.

He rubbed his fingers back and forth over the spot, and Cooper moaned and shuddered at every touch, nerves alight and cock drooling pre-cum. His balls grew tight and heavy with the need to come, until he couldn't take it anymore. "Nate?" he rasped, reaching out and clutching at Nate's shoulder.

When Nate lifted his head, his pupils were dark pools of want. "Yeah," he said, licking his lips. "Yeah."

He settled in the vee of Cooper's legs and slathered lube on his cock, notching the head against Cooper's arse. "I might not last long," he warned, eyes wide, then he pressed forward.

*Fuck.*

Nate was big, and Cooper could feel every thick inch of him as he nudged his way inside, rocking his hips and easing forward one gentle thrust at a time, making a space for himself. Nate's face was a picture of bliss, his mouth hanging open as he sank all the way inside. He stilled, his breath coming in shallow pants, giving Cooper time to adjust before he started to thrust in earnest.

It was overwhelming in all the best ways, and Cooper didn't think he'd last long either, not with the way Nate was nailing his prostate, snapping his hips forward, fucking into him with short, brutal strokes, filling him and lighting him up from the inside with every thrust.

As Nate picked up speed, Cooper's cock throbbed with the need to come and he jerked himself off furiously, every nerve coiling tighter and tighter until Nate pulled him back by the hips and thrust in deep, the new angle hitting all Cooper's sweet spots. Cooper came undone—arse clenching, back arching like a bowstring and fangs and claws exploding as he came all over himself.

Nate gave a low groan and fucked into him one last time, his body tensing before curling over Cooper and panting out his own release, his head hanging low.

Seeing him like that, Cooper was driven by an instinctive need to claim—to *own*—and he surged upward. He grasped Nate's head and tilted it to one side, managing to choke out, "Can I — " before Nate was nodding frantically.

His fangs sliced through the skin of Nate's throat with shocking ease.

Nate gave a high-pitched whine, eyes wide, and Cooper felt it — the bond between them snapping into place. It was heat and static electricity and champagne bubbles and the depths of the ocean on a hot summer's day all rolled into one. Running through it all, thrumming with life, was a shimmering silver core that couldn't be anything but Nate. It pulsed in his chest, warm and solid and impossible to ignore.

Nate's hand flew to his throat, then to his chest. "Fuck," he choked out. "Is that — "

Cooper could sense everything Nate was feeling through their bond, and it was a heady mix of awe, curiosity, excitement and shock — but one emotion stood out, overriding them all, lighting Nate up like a Christmas tree. It was the same one that surged through Cooper's own veins.

*Joy.*

* * * *

Cooper woke to the warm, steady rhythm of *mate mate mate* pulsing in his chest, and to fingers running through his hair. When he opened his eyes, Nate was gazing at him, and he could feel a thread of worry through their bond. "Hey, baby."

Nate gave a smile, but it was a poor effort. "We, um. Need to talk."

Panic flared, there and gone again before Nate's eyes widened and he pulled himself upright in bed, hand flying to his chest on instinct. "No! Not *that* kind of 'we need to talk.' Just practical shit. Am I moving to Sydney? Do you *want* me to move to Sydney? Because I feel like with the bond, distance would suck, but I can't just pick up and move next week, you know?"

Cooper propped himself up on one elbow and dragged Nate in for a kiss, and Nate responded, relaxing against him.

When Cooper pulled back, Nate's smile was more genuine. "That's cheating, distracting me from my freakout."

Cooper shrugged. "Did it work?"

"Well, yeah. But you didn't answer any of my questions."

Cooper settled his elbows on his knees and ran a hand through his sleep and sex-tousled hair. "Nate, I'll tell you what you told me. Whatever being your mate involves, I'm in. I want it all. I want *you.*"

"Smooth fucker," Nate muttered. He reached out and tangled their fingers together. "But we do need to make some plans, because my brain's a mess right now."

Cooper reached out and pulled Nate close, an arm around his shoulders. "How about this? We spend the rest of the week in the Swan Valley like we planned. We visit some wineries, eat some chocolate, fuck like bunnies and figure shit out."

"Figure shit out," Nate repeated. "Is that the kind of stellar problem-solving that got you where you are today?"

Cooper grinned, a lazy, fucked-out smile. "Baby, I can work out of Perth or Sydney. As long as we're together, it doesn't matter to me. I just meant we'd work out the nuts and bolts of it."

"That sounds like a pretty bloody perfect plan, then," Nate said. "Especially the fucking like bunnies part." He traced a hand over Cooper's pec, and Cooper could take a hint. He rolled them so Nate was underneath him and kissed him, tongues entwined and hands roaming over skin. The bond thrummed with shared satisfaction as they rutted against each other, unhurried. He slid his hand between them and jerked them both off, slow and lazy, until Nate's back arched and he came with a soft sigh, eyelashes fluttering against his cheeks and his mouth a perfect O. The sight was enough to have Cooper following right after.

He stayed there, face buried in the crook of Nate's neck until he'd caught his breath, then rolled off to the side and wiped his hand on a corner of the sheet.

He closed his eyes and floated. He had a vague awareness of a cool cloth wiping his belly and his hand, but after that he must have dozed, because the next thing he knew Nate was shaking him awake and was saying, "Wake up, sleepywolf."

When he opened his eyes, Nate was propped up on one elbow next to him, watching him. His hair was sleep-tousled, his cheeks were pink, and he was perfection. He was also grinning, like he had a secret and couldn't wait to share it.

"Hey," Cooper said, giving a lazy smile. "What's up?"

Nate beamed at him. "I had a revelation while you were napping, Coop."

"Oh?" Cooper reached out and brushed the hair away from Nate's forehead, unable to stop touching his mate.

"Yeah." Nate ran a fingertip through Cooper's chest hair, tracing patterns. "I'm guessing you own your house in Sydney?'

"It's an apartment, but yes. In Rozelle."

Nate nodded. "Uh-huh. And I live in a shitty fibro share house in Balga. So it occurred to me that it makes more sense for me to come to you."

Cooper's heart raced. "Really? Just like that?" The very thought of Nate in his space filled Cooper with warmth.

"Really," Nate said, wearing a wicked grin that made Cooper want to pin him down and ruin him. "Just like that. I mean, not *quite* just like that. I can't move to Sydney right now, because I'll need at least a month to sort my shit out. The lease isn't in my name, but I don't wanna be a dick to my housemate. And Sully needs time to find a new permanent offsider. And I need to pack, and to sell my ute and let Mum get used to the idea. So yeah, say a month." He creased his brow then bit his lip. "And, um. Is my sexy CEO mate willing to support me while I settle in and find a job?"

Cooper laughed. "Your sexy CEO mate would *love* to provide for you. In fact, you should know that I'm going to spoil you rotten. Sorry, but it's a werewolf thing."

Nate broke into a grin. "I think I can just about cope. So, a month? If you can wait that long?"

Cooper swallowed around a lump in his throat. His mate was coming *home*. "Sweetheart, I've waited thirty-eight years. I can wait another month, if I get to have you." He rolled over, pressing Nate into the mattress beneath him as he kissed him deep and filthy, then kissed his way up Nate's throat, revelling in the fact that Nate was *his*.

When they parted, Nate's face was flushed and his gaze was liquid heat. "Fuck," he said, his voice thick with want. "Maybe *I* can't wait a month. How does three weeks sound?"

Cooper's heart beat faster, and his inner wolf danced, delighted. "Perfect. You'll love it in Sydney, baby." Cooper kissed the shell of Nate's ear. "My apartment overlooks the bridge," he purred, "and my windows *are* werewolf rated."

"I can't wait," Nate said, eyes bright. "I mean, I'm sure I will love it, but at the risk of sounding clichéd, home is wherever you are." He blinked up at Cooper and wrinkled his nose. "Fuck, that was meant to sound romantic, but it was bloody awful, wasn't it?"

"It was shocking," Cooper agreed, smiling so hard that his face hurt. "Lucky for you, I love you anyway."

# Australian English Glossary

The author acknowledges the trademarked status and trademark owners of the following wordmarks mentioned in this work of fiction:

Balga: A suburb of Perth, Western Australia
Boardies: Board shorts, swimming shorts, swimming trunks
Doona: A duvet, comforter, or quilt
Fibro: Fibrous cement sheet, a popular building product in Australia that, prior to 1990 regulations, frequently contained asbestos.
Floreat: A suburb of Perth, Western Australia
Fluoro: Fluorescent, brightly coloured
HECS: Higher Education Contribution Scheme, a type of Australian student loan
Rashie: Rash guard, rash vest
Rort: To commit a scam or fraud
Singlet: Vest, tank top, sleeveless top
Smoko: Work break
Sunnies: Sunglasses
Thongs: Flip-flops
Tradie: A tradesman

# Want to see more from this author? Here's a taster for you to enjoy!

## Bad Boyfriends, Inc.: Awfully Ambrose
### Sarh Honey and Lisa Henry

*Excerpt*

The voice was loud and obnoxious, at odds with the restaurant's muted soundtrack of clinking cutlery, soft jazz and murmured conversation.

"Really appreciate you paying for dinner, Tom. I'm between opportunities right now but I'll be damned if I'm gonna take just any job and be a corporate drone. Better to take a free meal when I can get one, right?"

It was followed by a braying laugh that made Liam wince and want to drag his nails down a blackboard, because that would have been preferable to listening to this honking, snorting nightmare.

Liam prayed he wouldn't have to wait on whoever the loud idiot was, but judging by the smirk on his co-worker Judy's face, he had a sudden sinking certainty that the table was his. Sure enough, when he glanced over to check, there was Braying Man in the middle of his section — elbows on the table, wearing a backwards baseball cap and a flannel shirt, picking at his teeth.

The idiot caught Liam's eye and snapped his fingers. "Hey, man, can we get a bread basket or something? And booze. Lots of booze. Her old man's paying, so make it the good stuff." He winked, then gave Liam honest-to-God finger guns.

The guy was an utter dickhead, Liam decided. Still, part of the job was keeping his opinions to himself, so Liam made his way over to the table, face carefully impassive. His mask slipped for a split second when he recognized the girl who was gazing at Dickhead with something like worship. It was Kelly, who he shared a Marketing Communications class with at the University of Sydney, and the last time Liam had talked to her, she'd been dating someone completely different—a nice, if slightly scruffy, guitarist in a pub band. He wondered what had happened to him.

The other couple at the table had to be Kelly's parents. They were looking at the guy with a slightly confused expression on their faces, like he was one of those hairless cats, and they couldn't decide if they were fascinated or horrified by his existence.

Liam had to admit, Dickhead was objectively attractive when he was keeping his mouth shut. He could have been a model, with his well-muscled physique, dark hair and carefully sculpted stubble. He had a strong, straight nose, killer jawline, and even white teeth. He was just Liam's type—or would have been, if Liam dated.

Liam cleared his throat and did his best to pretend he didn't know anyone at the table as he said, "Welcome to Bayside. Would you like to order some drinks?"

Dickhead rolled his eyes. "Wow. I guess you weren't listening, huh? I mean, I *literally* just asked you to bring us good booze."

Liam kept his face pleasantly neutral—he'd had plenty of practice, working as a waiter in a high-end Sydney restaurant—and clarified, "What, specifically, would you like to drink, sir?" He made sure to address Kelly's father, since he was obviously the one footing the bill.

The man smiled gratefully and started to say, "I'd like a gin and tonic, and my wife will have—"

Arsehole interrupted. "Just give me a bottle of that Don Paragraph stuff"—as someone from a family of winemakers, Liam died a tiny death at the mangled pronunciation—"and the quicker the better, yeah?"

"I'll check if we have any *Dom Perignon* in stock, sir. How many glasses with that?" Liam asked through clenched teeth. God, he hoped they weren't celebrating Kelly's engagement to this douchebag.

Dude wrinkled his nose. "Just one. It's for me." He turned to Kelly and winked. "Gotta watch for extra calories in drinks if you wanna stay in shape, am I right, sweet pea?"

Liam waited for Kelly to rip the guy's balls off—he hoped literally, but he'd settle for metaphorically—because he knew she had a hell of a temper when she was wronged. He'd been on the receiving end of it during one disastrous group assignment. But Kelly just smiled like a Stepford Wife and murmured, "Yes, Ambrose."

Liam was pretty sure the shock on her father's face was mirrored on his own, but he schooled his features and nodded. Ambrose tilted a menu at Kelly's father. "This seafood platter's meant to be for two, but you're cool with me ordering it, right, Tom?"

Kelly's father cleared his throat. "Kelly's allergic to seafood."

"That's cool, I wasn't planning on sharing anyway," the dickhead—*Ambrose*—said with an easy grin that lit up his entire face and really, it wasn't fair that someone who was such a colossal arsehole could be so attractive.

But of course, that was how the world worked, right? Beautiful people got away with murder.

Liam turned back to the older man. "And the rest of your drinks order, sir?" he asked, taking petty satisfaction at the way Ambrose snorted and muttered under his breath.

"A gin and tonic for myself, and a glass of Connelly Cellars' Perfect Pinot," Tom said, and Liam suppressed the urge to preen, just like he did every time someone ordered one of his family's wines.

"Make mine a tonic water," Kelly said.

Liam blinked. *Wow, what happened to the girl who always claimed she'd never drink water because fish fucked in it?*

Something weird was going on, and whatever it was, Liam didn't like it. He especially didn't like that it was happening here at Bayside. People didn't come into Bayside wearing backwards caps and being dicks. Bayside had standards—standards that Liam was beginning to worry he might have to attempt to enforce. It had water views! You could see the Sydney Harbour Bridge from the wide dining room windows! It was both fancy and trendy, and it *always* made the list of the top ten places to eat in Sydney. Diners weren't supposed to wear flannel to Bayside, and Liam panicked quietly that he didn't know if the dress code was actually enforceable or not. Liam had only been working here for eight months, but it had never come up before. People usually treated Bayside like it was a special occasion, not three a.m. at the counter of Macca's.

"Good choice, babe. You know you're a sloppy drunk," Ambrose said, leaning in and patting Kelly's face. Then he hauled himself out of his chair, scratched his belly and farted. "I gotta go take a dump. I always shit when I'm out. Make someone else deal with that, am I right?" And with that Ambrose sauntered towards the bathrooms, leaving Kelly's parents staring after him open-mouthed.

Liam couldn't help himself. "Kelly —"

"Hi, Liam, I guess you've met my new boyfriend now!" Kelly cut in, following that with a tinkling laugh that was pitched a little high with nerves. "He's an entrepreneur."

Liam opened his mouth to ask what happened to Greg the bassist, but Kelly shot him a glare that said she would hunt him down and personally set his dick on fire if he said another word. Liam knew that look, so he shut his mouth, went to fetch drinks and said a prayer that he wouldn't have to be the one to clean the toilets at the end of the night. Frankly, he wouldn't have been surprised to learn that Ambrose had just decided to take a shit on the floor and stolen all the paper.

When Ambrose wandered back out again at last, he didn't walk straight back to his own table. Instead, he approached another table where a group of shiny and fashionable young women who were probably Instagram influencers or something were eating.

"Hi, ladies," he said. He put both hands on their table and leaned forward. "My name's Ambrose."

"Is he —?" Kelly's mother's mouth dropped open. "Oh my God."

"Ambrose is very sociable," Kelly said. "People love him."

A ticking vein in her father's temple called her a liar.

Liam saw the way that Tom started to strangle his linen napkin, and hurried over to the influencers' table. "Excuse me, sir," he said to Ambrose. "Can you please return to your own table?"

Ambrose gave him finger guns, and sauntered back over to join Kelly and her parents.

What the everlasting *fuck*? And Liam obviously wasn't the only one thinking it. Kelly's mum looked close to tears, and her dad looked half a heartbeat away from either a stroke or a homicide. In the event he actually did murder Ambrose, Liam decided to tell the police it was justified. Hell, at this point he'd probably give the guy an alibi. And the murder weapon. And a bucket of bleach to clean up the murder scene.

Kelly, though, just beamed at Ambrose like she was under some sort of spell. "I missed you, boo." She blew him a kiss.

Ambrose shrugged. "Have we ordered yet? I'm starving. Service here is soooo slow," he said loudly, stretching his arms over his head and attracting stares from the other tables. "Probably can't get decent staff."

Liam seethed and wondered if he and Tom could come to some sort of agreement regarding mutual alibis and body disposal. The walk-in freezer out the back would be a good place to store a corpse while they figured out their next step.

Liam woodenly went through the specials, which nobody ever ordered anyway, then took their menus back and excused himself. He'd only made it a few steps away from the table when the obnoxious click of someone's fingers pulled him back again.

"Garçon!"

Ambrose. Of-fucking-course.

"Hey, change Kelly's order to a garden salad," Ambrose said. He grinned at Kelly. "We don't want you getting too chunky, right, babe?"

That vein in Tom's temple looked about ready to pop. "Kelly can eat what she bloody well likes," he hissed in an undertone.

"A salad sounds great, actually," Kelly said. "Ambrose knows what's best. Babe, tell them about your business ideas."

Ambrose straightened up, his eyes gleaming. "Have you guys heard of multi-level marketing?"

This time it was Liam's jaw that dropped. Kelly was a *business major*.

"So," Ambrose said to Kelly's stone-faced parents, "what you do is, you have a product, and you recruit people to sell it for you. They're called a downline. Like, some people say that it's predatory and cult-like, but I've been in a cult, and ha! You won't fool me like that twice! Well, three times. Did you bring your chequebook, Tom? I mean, I can take cash if you want to get on board too, I guess. Like, what do you think? Five grand?"

Liam stared at Kelly for a moment, wondering who the fuck she even was, then escaped to the kitchen to put in their orders before he finally snapped. He managed to resist the urge to tell the chef to spit on the seafood, but it was a close-run thing.

\* \* \* \*

Things hadn't really improved by dessert. As the level in his bottle of Dom had dropped, Ambrose had become steadily more obnoxious and his volume levels had risen—Liam had been able to hear him from all the way across the restaurant.

He came out with such gems as, "No, I'd never want kids. I want my partner's sole focus to be me, and they'd need to work so we can afford for me to pursue my dreams. Plus, y'know, I've banged a few cougars and I can tell you now, the body never quite bounces back, does it?" Here he turned to Kelly's mum. "You know what I'm talking about, right, Jeanette?"

"Jesus Christ," said Alastair softly in Liam's ear.

Alastair was one of the other waiters working tonight. He hadn't quite believed Liam's "I have the worst fucking customer ever" story when Liam had told the first part of it in the kitchen between courses, and he'd come to see for himself.

"I know, right?" Liam murmured back. "Wait until he calls me 'garçon' again."

"Fuck off, he did not."

Liam nodded grimly. "Snapped his fucking fingers and everything."

Alastair shook his head. "I don't know why you even put up with this shit. Why do you work here again? Aren't your parents loaded?"

Liam suppressed a sigh. "They own a winery. It's not the same thing. Besides, I'm twenty-three. I can pay my own way through uni. I don't need my mum giving me pocket money."

Alastair looked sceptical. "I guess."

As they watched, Ambrose started waving his hands animatedly. "Yeah," he said at a volume level more suited to a dance club than a restaurant, "I'm definitely too good to settle for any old job. I mean, look at me. I've *modelled*, for Christ's sake." He pulled his shirt up to show off a lean torso and sculpted abs. Liam might have been impressed, except he suspected that the only reason Ambrose was so fit was because he was constantly running away from people who wanted to punch him in the face.

"I'm dating a *model*, Mum," Kelly said. "Aren't I lucky?"

Tom looked unimpressed. "Yeah? I've never seen your face anywhere."

Ambrose gave a sheepish grin. "Well, I *say* modelling, but it wasn't exactly mainstream. And it didn't exactly feature my face as the main attraction. It was more off-grid, online, pay-per-view, take-yourself-in-hand kind of work, you get me?"

There was stunned silence. "You mean…?" Jeanette started.

"I guess you old people would call it porn, yeah. It was pretty successful, too." He reached for his phone. "Wanna see?"

"No, we bloody well don't," Tom snapped.

Something in his tone must have gotten through because Ambrose just shrugged and said, "I'll leave it up to your imagination. Or you can ask Kell." He gave a filthy wink to Jeanette, along with the inevitable finger guns.

Liam checked his watch and willed them to leave. Surely two hours was enough of this torture? He was relieved to see that Ambrose was standing, possibly in preparation for departure, but his heart sank when Ambrose cleared his throat, shook out his arms, and declared to anyone who was listening, "I'm gonna do a magic trick!"

With a determined set to his chin, he grabbed the corner of the tablecloth.

"Oh, Jesus," Liam groaned, and sprinted across the room. "Sir!" he bellowed, not caring how he looked, "please don't attempt to remove the tablecloth! It never works!"

"It'll work for me! It's gonna be amazing!" Ambrose insisted. And with that he pulled at the cloth, which, instead of sliding out from under the crockery in a dazzling display of finesse, dragged everything along with it, sending plates, glasses and cutlery crashing onto the floor and a glass of red wine into Jeanette's lap.

Ambrose stared at the wreckage, and Liam could have sworn he was genuinely shocked.

"Well, *fuck*," he said loudly. "That didn't happen on YouTube."

# About the Author

Sarah started life in New Zealand. She came to Australia for a working holiday, loved it and never left. She lives in Western Australia with her partner, two cats, two dogs and a life-sized replica TARDIS. She spends half her time at a day job and the rest of her time reading and writing about clueless men falling in love, with a dash of humour and spice thrown in along the way.

Her proudest achievements include having adult kids who will still be seen with her in public, the ability to make a decent sourdough loaf, and knowing all the words to *Bohemian Rhapsody*. She has co-authored both the Bad Boyfriends, Inc and the Adventures in Aguillon series with Lisa Henry. *Socially Orcward*, the third book in the Aguillon series, was runner-up in the Best Asexual Book category in 2021's Rainbow Awards.

Sarah loves to hear from readers. You can find her contact information, website details and author profile page at https://www.pride-publishing.com

PUBLISHING

Sign up for our newsletter and find out about all our romance book releases, eBook sales and promotions, sneak peeks and FREE romance books!

Milton Keynes UK
Ingram Content Group UK Ltd.
UKHW040650140923
428670UK00001B/41